Wedge of Fear

Wedge of Fear

Eugene M. Gagliano

Crystal Publishing LLC
Fort Collins, Colorado

Wedge of Fear

Edited by Bonnie Walker and Patricia Phillips

Cover art by Erika Parker Rogers
Cover design by Lotus Design www.lotusdesign.biz

Published by Crystal Publishing, LLC
Fort Collins, Colorado

ISBN 978-1-942624-38-7
Library of Congress Control Number: 2018944097

Also by the author

C is for Cowboy, a Wyoming Alphabet
Four Wheels West, a Wyoming Number Book
V is for Venus Flytrap, a Plant Alphabet
My Teacher Dances on the Desk
Little Wyoming
The Magic Box
Angel's Landing
Booger
Dee and the Mammoth

For my grandchildren: Kyla, Dakota, Connor, Bella, Ethan, and Lexi, who are blessed to have loving mothers and fathers.

Love,
Grandpa

Rough Start

"Stop treating me like a little kid!"

"Tony, don't talk to your mother that way." Dad pointed a finger at him.

"But, Dad, nobody in sixth grade has their mom go with them to school on their first day." Tony pushed strands of hair out of his eyes and sighed. He placed his empty cereal bowl on the kitchen counter.

"I just want you to get off to a good start. This is a new school," Mom said, rinsing out a dish. "We've only been in Wyoming a week, and you don't know anybody yet."

"I'll be fine, Mom," Tony said, even though his stomach tightened with the thought of going to a new school. What if the kids didn't like him? What if they made fun of him because he was from New York? Could he take care of himself?

Tony's broad-shouldered dad, Gene, reached down and wrapped his arms around his wife's tiny waist. "Frances, Tony will be fine." He winked at Tony.

"But, Gene, what if..." Mom looked down and rubbed her hands on her skirt.

"He'll be all right," Dad whispered into her ear.

Tony smiled. "I'll be okay. I'll make new friends."

"Well, I suppose. But make sure you're careful with your new jeans. Money is tight now, with moving and all. I can't afford to buy you new clothes the way that you're growing." She reached over to adjust his shirt collar.

Tony pulled away. "Mom, don't."

"Tony, you'd better get going so you're not late." Dad placed his arm around Tony's shoulder. "I'll see you tonight. Good luck."

"Thanks, Dad. Bye, Mom."

"Give me a kiss before you go." Mom hugged him tight and kissed him on the cheek. Hugging and kissing were a natural part of Tony's Italian family life. He knew Mom loved him—maybe too much.

The school was only five blocks away, but Tony hurried. He didn't want to be late. The September sky burned blue above him, and a gentle breeze rustled the shiny green leaves of the cottonwoods. He couldn't believe how blue the sky was compared to the overcast sky he was used to seeing. The air smelled crisp and clean, unlike the city air he was used to. This was Wyoming, his new home, and things were different. What would his new school be like? He bit his lip thinking about sixth grade. Tony looked at his watch— only ten minutes left to get to Clear Creek School.

Feeling anxious, Tony decided to run the rest of the way. He sped past the ball field and over the bridge crossing a creek. That must be the creek the school was named after. The red brick school sprawled out before him. The main building had two floors and a bell tower on the roof. He saw only one large tree. That was too bad. Many old maple and elm trees had shaded his old school. He used to like joking around with his friends and eating his lunch under their shade.

Tony ran across the asphalt playground, still looking at the lone tree and wondering if it was good for climbing. He felt his foot slip on some loose gravel, and before he could do anything to catch his balance, he had tumbled to the ground.

His scraped hands stung. Tony stood and looked at his bruised and bleeding knees that now poked out of the holes in his new jeans. Great. Mom would have a fit. He could feel tears welling up in his eyes.

Though the playground had looked empty moments before, several students now gathered around him to witness his humiliation.

"You're the new kid from back East. I've heard about you," a big, blonde girl said, snapping her gum. "Don't you people know how to run without killing yourselves?"

Tony blushed like Roma tomatoes. He looked at the girl rooted in front of him with her hands on her hips. She looked older than him. And bigger, too. Small and thin, Tony was dwarfed by this giant who stared down at him. He hated being small. Tony pushed his unruly black hair away from his face. He tried to smile but couldn't think of anything to say.

"Hey, Regina. Leave him alone."

Tony turned to see a boy with freckles and a big grin. His reddish-brown hair stuck out from under a cowboy hat, and he wore cowboy boots. He looked like the real Wyoming deal. He stood a little taller than Tony, but he looked friendly.

The cowboy stuck a hand out. "Hi, I'm Jed."

Tony grabbed the hand and felt a real smile spread across his face. "I'm Tony."

"He's from back East," Regina sneered. She cracked her knuckles.

Jed glanced at her. "So what, Regina? Get lost."

Regina snorted and tromped off.

"Don't pay any attention to her." Jed scowled. "She thinks she's somebody special."

Tony looked down at his blood-speckled hands. He didn't know what to do.

Jed's eyes glanced from Tony's hands to his ripped jeans. "Looks like you crashed," he said. "I'll show you to the nurse's office."

Tony, still at a loss for words, followed Jed into the building and down a long brick hallway.

"Who's your teacher?" Jed asked.

"Mr. Brunswick," Tony said, glad to have something to talk about. "What's he like?"

"Better than old lady Cranwell." Jed chuckled. He pointed at a door with a shiny plaque that read NURSE. "Better hurry up—class starts soon. I'll see you later."

By the time Tony finished with the nurse, classes had started. The thought of having to walk into a full classroom, where everyone was sure to stare at him because he was late, made him walk even slower down the locker-lined hallway toward the door labeled MR. BRUNSWICK. Tony entered a room full of unfamiliar faces, except for Regina and Jed. Mr. Brunswick, a tall man with short blond hair and a funny mustache, greeted Tony with a smile. He invited Tony to sit down in the only empty desk in the room, which of course just happened to be next to Regina. Tony slipped into the desk, his stomach flipping.

Despite his rough start, the morning passed quickly. Mr. Brunswick handed out books, covered rules, and assigned lockers. Regina crossed her eyes and stuck her tongue out at Tony whenever she could, but Tony ignored her as much as possible.

At lunch, Jed invited Tony to eat with him and his friend Randy. The basement lunchroom had fold-up tables with attached seats, just like at his old school, except these were blue instead of green. The students bought lunches of beans and franks with peanut butter bars for dessert. It was one of his favorite lunches at his old school.

"So, what's it like back East?" Jed asked Tony.

"Well..." Tony thought for a moment. "There's lots of people and lots of traffic."

"What do you think of Wyoming?" Randy asked. He pushed his glasses up on his pudgy nose.

"Not lots of people. And not lots of traffic." Randy and Jed laughed, which made Tony smile back. "I've only been here for about a week, and I haven't had a chance to see much. My dad says we might go up to the mountains for a picnic this weekend."

Jed nodded approvingly. "Does your dad hunt?" He wiped his mouth with the back of his hand.

"No."

"Ever been out to a ranch?" Jed asked, biting his nail.

"No." Tony took two big bites of his hot dog and gulped down some milk. Then, he wolfed down a handful of potato chips.

"Maybe you could come out to our ranch sometime. It's just twelve miles south of town."

Tony's mouth opened wide. "You live twelve miles from school?" He stuffed some more chips into his mouth.

"That's nothing," Randy said. "I live fifteen miles east of town."

"Wow! Fifteen miles!" Everyone at his old school had lived more or less within walking distance from their school. But he would have had to take the bus to get to middle school this year, if he'd stayed in New York. "I'd like to visit a real ranch. Jed, do you have horses and stuff like that?"

"We've got a lot of horses."

"You're lucky." Tony stuffed some beans into his mouth.

"Tony, you hungry or something?" Randy said.

"Look at how skinny he is. Of course he's hungry," Jed teased.

Jed's remark embarrassed Tony, but he tried not to let it show. He ate all the time, but he just couldn't put on any weight. Dad told him it was because he was growing.

"Hey, Tony," Randy said. "You're from the East. You must like seafood?"

"Sure."

"Okay. Close your eyes." Randy grinned at Jed.

When Randy told him to open his eyes, Tony scowled. Randy had his mouth opened wide. His tongue stuck out, displaying a glob of chewed frank and beans. Jed and Randy roared with laughter.

"Gross!" Tony grinned.

"You said you liked to see food," Randy said. "So, I just chewed up some food for you to see. Pretty neat, huh?"

Tony laughed. "Neat. But that's nothing." He paused. "One time a guy at my old school sneezed spaghetti out his nose."

"Oh, gross!" Jed exclaimed. "Did spaghetti really come out his nose?"

"Yep. It was the most disgusting thing I ever saw."

Randy laughed and laughed. "You're okay, Tony." He gave Tony a friendly punch in the arm.

"Yep, you're okay." Jed agreed with a nod of his head.

The rest of the day passed quickly. Regina tried to trip Tony when he went up to sharpen his pencil and continued to make weird faces at him, but before Tony knew it, school was over. He had decided Mr. Brunswick might be all right, and he really liked Jed and Randy.

He wished he could ride the bus home with Jed. Tony left the school grounds wondering how he was going to explain the torn jeans to Mom…if she would even let him. Somebody called his name. He turned to see Regina and some other girls behind him.

"Hey, Tony!" Regina bellowed again. "You got a girlfriend?"

Tony hesitated. "Uh…no."

"Want to be my boyfriend?" Regina flexed her biceps.

"No way!" Who would want a big-mouthed giant for a girlfriend?

"I thought you city kids were great lovers," Regina teased. "What's the matter?"

"Leave me alone!"

Tony walked faster, but he could still hear Regina and the other girls laughing. Why didn't she leave him alone? Was it just because he was the new kid? He would stay as far away from her as he could.

As he continued to walk home, he thought about his new friend Jed and about visiting him at his ranch. Wow! A real western ranch. He couldn't wait to tell his mom and dad, and then, he remembered his torn jeans. Mom was probably going to throw a fit. He slowed down and thought about what he would say.

When Tony arrived home, Mom greeted him at the door. She smiled until she noticed the torn jeans. Her eyes flashed.

"Anthony Eugene, what did you do?" Mom placed her delicate hands over her mouth.

Tony sat down on the blue living room sofa. "Well, I was…"

Mom stood next to him patting down her red and white apron. "You know we can't afford to buy you new clothes all the time."

"I didn't do it on purpose." Tony leaned back against the high-backed sofa and stuck his hands deep into the pockets of his new jeans. He wasn't in the mood for another lecture.

"I told you this morning to be careful and look at you. I knew I should have gone with you. Did you get hurt?"

Tony looked down at the gray carpeting. "Just some scratches. The nurse took care of it."

Mom sighed. "Are you sure you're all right?

Tony rolled his eyes. "Yes, Mom."

"You sure, because…"

Tony jumped up and headed toward his room. "I'm okay. Just leave me alone!"

Tony ran to his bedroom and slammed the door shut. He hoped his mom wouldn't follow him. He could take care of himself. Why couldn't she leave him alone?

Daggers in the Sky

On Saturday morning, the sky was a brilliant cobalt blue, and the air smelled fresh as Tony and his parents headed up highway 16 into the Big Horn Mountains that towered above Buffalo.

"We're finally going up to the mountains," Dad said. He looked over his shoulder at Tony in the backseat of the car. "I can't believe we've already been here for three weeks. I think a picnic is just what the doctor ordered."

"Can we hike?" Tony asked.

"Sure. Keep your eye out for deer. My boss told me the deer graze along the roadside."

"I hope the flies aren't bad." Mom scowled. "I hate flies."

"Come on now, Frances. Flies don't eat much."

Tony laughed at his Dad's remark, and Mom rolled her eyes.

The base of the Big Horn Mountains was a ten-minute drive from Tony's house. Highway 16 wound like a snake up toward the peaks dusted with snow. The warm air blowing in the windows began to smell like pine. It played with his hair. He could almost taste the watermelon that lay at his feet. The radio played an unfamiliar western song. Country music was all Dad liked to listen to lately on the radio. He wished he had brought his iPhone with him.

"Gene, can we please turn the radio off? That country music drives me crazy," Mom adjusted her silver chain necklace.

"Yeah, Dad. I don't care for it either." Tony scratched the back of his head.

"I kind of like it. Sort of grows on you."

"You mean like green mold on cheese?" Tony laughed.

Dad laughed, too. "Okay, I'll turn it off."

The Big Horn Mountains stretched before him like a panoramic painting. It was almost too beautiful to be real. The forest seemed endless, and the mountain peaks appeared more beautiful with every curve in the highway.

"Frances, hold on!" Dad shouted as he slammed on the brakes.

"Gene, watch out!" Mom yelled, grabbing the dashboard in front of her.

Tony's seatbelt caught him as he flew forward.

Mom closed her eyes and let out a scream.

"Holy cow! I never saw the deer until it was in front of me," Dad said.

Tony took a deep breath and looked out the front window. A large-eared mule deer ambled up the mountainside, never giving the car a second glance.

"Oh, I see it now." What if they had hit it and the car had veered off the edge of mountain road? His stomach did a flip.

"Goodness gracious! Tony, are you all right?" Mom rubbed the creases in her forehead and adjusted her glasses. Her face was flushed.

Tony checked his seatbelt to make sure it was tight. "I'm okay."

"I can't believe it just darted out in front of us," Mom said. She held her hand over her heart and took a deep breath.

"Calm down, Frances. Nobody got hurt. The deer don't know any better."

"Calm down? We could've all been killed!" Mom gestured wildly with her hands. "You want me to calm down? Really, Gene, sometimes I just don't understand you."

Dad sighed and continued to drive up the winding highway. Tony slumped back into his seat. He stared out the window at the snowy peaks in the distance. Why did Mom always get so hysterical? She made him nervous and afraid.

Dad pulled off the main highway and entered the Hunter Creek Picnic Area. Three empty, weathered picnic tables waited in a grassy area in the noonday sun.

"Looks like we have the place to ourselves," Tony said.

"Hard to believe. I'm used to wall-to-wall people."

Mom eyed the nearby outhouse. "I'm used to indoor plumbing."

Dad parked the car in the dappled shade of a clump of aspen trees. Mom made Tony unpack the car.

"Remember, Tony, watch out for snakes," Mom said.

"Mom, I told you already. Jed says there aren't any rattlesnakes up here."

Mom surveyed the picnic area. "Well, it never hurts to be careful. And stay out of the water."

"Frances, Tony and I are going to take a short walk before lunch."

"Okay, but don't go far," Mom said. She shooed a fly away. "Lunch will be ready in a few minutes. I'm going to set a nice table and finish making the sandwiches. I didn't want to serve you soggy egg salad sandwiches."

Tony and Dad followed the shady path along the stream. A red squirrel chattered above, and the pungent smell of pine filled the air. Bright green mosses like carpet samples clung to the rocks right down to the edge of the water. The swirling stream sparkled and bubbled downhill. Tony couldn't resist sticking his hand into the clear water.

"Dad, can I take off my shoes and socks and wade?"

Dad looked over his shoulder toward the picnic area. "Don't let Mom see you."

Tony kicked off his shoes and yanked off his socks.

"As a matter of fact, I think I'll join you."

Tony stepped into the frigid water, followed by Dad.

"Whoa, it's freezing!" Tony shuddered.

Dad swished the water with his foot. "Boy, I'll say. How can the fish stand it?"

"Funny, Dad."

"Hey, Tony."

"What?"

"That's what," Dad said, splashing him.

Water dripped down Tony's face.

Tony reached down and splashed Dad. "You asked for it." The frigid water pasted Dad's blue plaid shirt to his broad chest.

"Okay, okay. Enough." Dad laughed and covered his face with his hands. "We're even."

Mom appeared from behind them. "Anthony Eugene! What did I tell you?"

"Come on, Frances. We're just having a little fun," Dad said. "The water's not deep."

Mom shook her head. "Gene, you're the adult. You should know better."

When Tony walked out of the water, he heard a big splash.

"Gene!" Mom shouted clasping her hands. "Are you all right?"

Tony turned and saw Dad sitting in the water. He had a sheepish grin on his face.

"Way to go, Dad."

"Don't just stand there, Tony." Dad laughed. "Give me a hand."

As Dad dripped his way back to the picnic table, Mom scolded him again. Dad changed into a pair of extra overalls he had in the trunk of the car. He tried to make light of the matter, but Mom wasn't happy.

"Don't complain to me when you start sniffling and sneezing." She opened a jar of Tony's favorite dill pickles. "A fine example you set for your son."

"Frances, you need to lighten up. I'll be fine."

An old dented pickup truck loaded with junk rumbled up to the outhouse, blowing a curtain of dust toward the picnic table. Mom swished the dust away with her hand. A big blonde woman wearing tight red shorts hopped out of the truck and raced to the outhouse. A burly, bearded man dressed in dirty, torn jeans stepped out the driver's side of the truck, followed by a large, black dog. The man spat on the ground and belched. The dog ran over to the picnic table and nuzzled Mom's leg.

"Get away from me," Mom said, shooing the dog away.

Dad called to the dog, "Come here, boy." He held his hand out, palm side up, and let the dog sniff it. Then, he pet the sleek black coat over and over. "You're a good old boy."

Mom bristled. "Gene, you're getting your hand all dirty."

Dad just shook his head and looked over at the truck.

"Rowdy, get over here," a familiar voice shouted from the cab of the truck.

Tony turned and stared, mouth hanging open. The truck door opened again and out plopped Regina, grinning from ear to ear. What was she doing here?

"Hey, Tony. I think my dog likes your dad." Regina, dressed in bib overalls and work boots, marched over to the picnic table like she was in charge. She snorted. "Come on, Rowdy. We don't want to scare anybody, now do we?" She snatched the dog by the collar and lumbered back to the truck.

"Hurry up!" the bearded man shouted toward the outhouse with a scowl. He jumped back into the pickup, and Regina and Rowdy followed. The outhouse door slammed, and the woman hopped back into the truck. In a flurry of dust, it sped away up the road.

"Who was that?" Mom asked.

"A girl from school," Tony said. He passed Dad the chips.

"She seems tough," Dad said.

Tony shrugged. She was tough and about as nice as a rattlesnake. Her dad looked kind of mean, too.

"They weren't very friendly," Mom said.

Dad shrugged his shoulders but said nothing.

After lunch, Tony wanted to hike up the road. Dad thought that was a great idea. Even Mom agreed. She wanted to get away from the flies that had discovered the picnic lunch and go see the wildflowers.

Tony led the way up the rutted dirt road that passed the Hunter Creek Ranger Station. The sun shone hot, but billowy gray clouds rose above the trees.

"I'm out of breath. Must be the change in elevation," Dad said, wiping sweat from his brow.

"We'd better not go too far," Mom said. She adjusted her glasses. "It looks like a storm is coming."

"We'll be all right, Frances. We're not going far."

"Dad, wouldn't it be neat to camp in the mountains?"

"I'd do it, but your mom doesn't like camping."

Mom flicked a bug from her arm. "You can say that again."

"Jed said that sometimes I might be able to go camping with him and his dad."

"I don't know about that, Tony," Mom said. "The mountains can be dangerous."

Tony rolled his eyes. "Mom, you think driving to the store is dangerous."

"Tony, you're too young to understand. I don't want anything to happen to you." She clutched her hands to her heart. "Losing Joey was enough," she whispered.

"Please, Frances, not now. Let's not spoil the day with sad memories."

Tony stared at his mom in surprise. She rarely mentioned that name.

Mom wiped a tear from her eye. "I'm sorry, but I can't help how I feel."

Joey, Joey, Joey. Tony couldn't even remember his brother, but because of Joey's accident, Mom wouldn't let him do anything. The memory of Joey hung over him like a dark cloud, threatening to make his life miserable.

"Tony, look." Dad pointed to a deer half hidden in a grove of aspen trees.

"I've never been this close to a deer in the wild," Tony said. He stared into its gentle face and liquid brown eyes.

"Isn't it beautiful?" Mom whispered.

Then, with a flick of its tail, the deer darted off into the trees.

Tony and his parents followed the winding road. Purple and yellow wildflowers embroidered its edges. The scent of pine wafted through the air on a cooling breeze that tousled his hair. It seemed to tickle the aspen leaves, which already hinted of the gold of autumn. He wished he had brought his sketchpad. Tony reached out and grabbed a spruce bough. It looked soft, but the needles pricked his hand. He noticed sticky sap oozing from some of the pine trees and the glint of an aluminum can tossed by the side of the road. Why did people litter in such a beautiful place? He picked up the can to deposit it later in the trash.

Then, the sun disappeared behind the clouds and the breeze picked up. It felt cool, like a wet towel placed on a feverish forehead. A dagger of lightning severed the sky, followed by a tremendous crash. He jumped.

Dad stopped abruptly. His eyebrows furrowed deeply, and he quickly turned around. "We'd better head back to the car."

Mom shivered. "I told you a storm was coming."

"Yes, dear. I know."

The sky grew darker as lightning stabbed the blackness. Rain started to fall.

Mom started to run. "Hurry, before we're all killed."

Tony shivered as another bolt of lightning arced across the sky. He bit his lower lip. Lightning had always frightened him. The rain turned into small pellets of hail, which grew into white marbles as he and his parents raced to the car.

"OW!" The hail hit Tony in a flurry. He could hardly see. By the time he jumped into the car, the air had become a sheet of white. The roar of ice hitting the car was deafening. Tony curled up in the back seat.

"Tony, are you all right?" Mom shouted, removing her glasses.

"I guess so."

"Boy, that storm came up fast," Dad yelled above the din of crashing hail. "If that hail gets any larger, it'll ruin the car."

"I tried to warn you," Mom said.

Dad glared at Mom. "Yes, Frances."

"You see, Tony. I told you the mountains could be dangerous," said Mom, finally finding a tissue in her purse to dry her glasses. "You should listen to me."

Tony slumped deeper into the backseat of the car. He knew the mountains could be dangerous. But what if Jed invited him to go camping? Mom would say no for sure. Maybe Mom was right. What would he do if a storm came up while he was camping?

The Note

"Pssst. Pssst," Regina said, waving a folded piece of paper under her desk. Through the classroom window, the early morning sun turned her hair to gold, as if she wore a halo. It should have given her horns instead.

Tony looked at Regina. Why was she giving him a note? He ignored her.

"Come on, take it," she whispered, pushing the note toward him.

He reached over and took the note. Tony unfolded it and read, MR. BRUNSWICK IS A JERK!

Tony glared at Regina. She gave him an innocent smile and raised her chubby hand.

"Mr. Brunswick. Tony's passing notes," she said.

"Tony, let me see the note." Mr. Brunswick placed a math book down on his desk.

Tony stiffened and clenched his fists. He could feel his face turning red. "But I didn't..." Tony was afraid to say that Regina wrote the note. Who knew what she might do to him? But he didn't want Mr. Brunswick to think he didn't like him. Frustrated, he bit his lip and fidgeted in his chair.

"Just bring it here, please."

"Yes, sir."

He brought the note up to Mr. Brunswick. Tony plunged his fists deep into his pockets and glared at Regina. Mr. Brunswick looked puzzled as he read the note.

"Tony, I'm surprised at you." He frowned. "I want to talk to you after school."

Tony nodded his head in agreement and hurried back to his desk. He slid into his seat. Regina smiled at him with folded hands, looking innocent as an angel. Tony gritted his teeth. He wanted to pull every blond hair out of her head, one handful at a time.

At recess, Regina and a group of giggling girls walked up to Tony.

"You shouldn't write notes in class. And you shouldn't get caught," she said with a smirk.

Tony scowled. "Regina."

"What?" Regina placed her hands on her hips.

"Never mind." Tony clenched his teeth and stomped off.

"Hey, Tony!" Jed called from across the playground.

Tony shuffled over to Jed.

"I think Regina likes you. I heard her say that you have beautiful brown eyes." Jed grinned. "I saw her pass you the love note."

"Love note. Give me a break," Tony said. "I hate her guts."

"If you say so." Jed jumped up on the monkey bars and began to swing. "Are you ready to go camping?"

"Yep, if Mom doesn't change her mind. What did your dad say to her?" Tony leaned against the monkey bars. "She looked relieved when she hung up the phone, but I didn't dare ask."

"You told me she probably wouldn't let you go because she's afraid that you might get hurt. My dad told her he was a member of the Search and Rescue Team."

Tony's mouth opened wide. "Is he?"

"He sure is," Jed swung back and forth. "He's saved lots of people."

Tony sighed in relief. "Well, I guess he saved me," Tony said, remembering how excited he had been when his mom told him he could go. "Where are we going to camp?" His eyes opened wide with anticipation. "Is it far from here? When are we leaving? Will it take long to get there?"

"Take it easy, Tony."

"I can't help it. I've never camped before. Do you think we'll see any bears?"

"Maybe."

Tony bit his lower lip. He'd heard stories on the news about bear attacks in the mountains.

"We're going up to West Ten Sleep Lake. It takes about an hour to get there. You'll need to bring warm clothes. It gets cold at night. Might even snow this time of year," Jed said.

"Do you really think we might see a bear?"

"Don't worry. If we do, I'll let you take care of it." Jed chuckled and climbed to the top of the monkey bars.

Tony felt his stomach roll. "Right." He could take care of himself, but he didn't know if he could handle a bear. "I still can't believe my mom's letting me go."

"We'll probably leave after school gets out on Friday."

"I can hardly wait." He climbed to the top of the monkey bars.

"Hey, Tony. Did I tell you that I helped my Aunt Billie butcher chickens last night?" He looked at Tony as if waiting for a reaction.

"Butcher chickens!" Tony grimaced.

"They're just chickens, Tony." Jed shook his head. "My aunt whacks the head off with a butcher knife. The chicken flops around without its head and finally drops dead." Jed looked Tony in the eye. "Then, we put the chicken into a pot of boiling water, hang it up, and pluck the feathers. That's the smelly part."

"That's gross, Jed."

"That's how you do it."

Tony didn't ever think he could do that. Suddenly, the thought of fried chicken sickened him.

"What did you do last night?" Jed asked.

"Not much, but my nana called."

Jed swung on the monkey bar. "Who?"

"My nana. You know, my grandmother."

"Oh."

"She might be coming out to visit us this Christmas. I hope so. She used to live across the street from us. Nana's funny. She likes to play cards, and she laughs a lot." Tony jumped to the ground. "Nana always has something for me. She gave me an iPhone as a going away present."

"My grandma died when I was little."

Tony didn't know what to say to that. The memory of Joey sprang to his mind, but he didn't say anything.

The recess bell rang, and Tony and Jed trudged back to class. Tony walked past Regina, who had her foot stuck out in the aisle. He tripped over her foot and fell flat on his face. The classroom exploded into laughter. When Tony stood, he could feel the blood burning in his cheeks. Through his glasses, Mr. Brunswick peered at him with a frown.

"What's going on, Tony?"

"Sorry, Tony," Regina said loudly.

"Nothing, Mr. Brunswick." Tony sat at his desk.

"Class, let me have your attention," Mr. Brunswick said. "Today, I'm going to give you a chance to draw anything you want. I'd like to see what you can do. Maybe there's a future artist among you. I'm going to play some background music while you draw. Anyone here like classical music?"

Nobody raised their hands.

"I thought so," Mr. Brunswick said. "I'll play some anyway. You might like this. It's Dvorak's *New World Symphony.*" Mr. Brunswick gave everyone a sheet of good drawing paper. "I'm going to display the best drawings on the bulletin board in the front of the room."

"Mr. Brunswick, may I draw a picture of a horse?" one girl asked.

"Yes. You can draw anything you want." Mr. Brunswick adjusted his glasses.

"Can I draw a picture of the principal in his underwear?" Regina asked.

Mr. Brunswick frowned. Everyone in the class laughed, except Tony. He glared at Regina. What was her problem?

"Have you seen the principal in his underwear, Regina?" Mr. Brunswick asked.

"Well, no." Regina blushed and squirmed in her seat.

"Then, I suggest you draw something else," Mr. Brunswick said. "Something you're familiar with."

Regina shrugged her shoulders and stared at her paper. Mr. Brunswick winked at Tony. Maybe Mr. Brunswick knew that he didn't write the note. Tony smiled back. He liked Mr. Brunswick.

Mr. Brunswick let everyone share their picture when they were finished. Jed drew a picture of an elk. Regina drew a picture of a horse that looked like a big dog. Everyone laughed at Regina's picture until Mr. Brunswick reminded them of their manners. Tony drew a mountain scene that made his classmates ooh and aah.

"Where did you learn to draw like that?" Mandy asked.

"You're GOOD," Randy said.

"How did you do that?" Jed asked and turned his paper over.

Tony didn't know what to say.

"It's not that great," Regina said. She wiped her nose with the back of her hand. "It's just some mountains and a bunch of trees."

"It's better than your dog," Randy said.

Regina puffed up. "It's a horse, Randy Rat."

"That's enough," Mr. Brunswick said. "Tony, have you had art lessons?"

"No, sir. I just like to draw. I draw a lot at home."

"Maybe you could bring some more of your drawings to school and share them with the class."

Mr. Brunswick smiled broadly at Tony. "You're very talented."

Tony felt good inside. He smiled, sat up straight, and held his head a little higher. Mr. Brunswick thought he was talented. Everyone had liked his drawing, except Regina. Who cared what she thought? He couldn't wait to tell Mom and Dad.

After everyone else was dismissed for the day, Mr. Brunswick called Tony up to the front of the room. Tony clasped his hands behind him, lowered his head, and slowly approached the teacher's desk.

Mr. Brunswick stared at him for a moment. "Tony, I know you didn't write the note. Sometimes students can be mean and try to get others into trouble. Usually the kids who do mean things are very unhappy. Sometimes they just want attention, even if it's negative attention. Do you understand what I'm saying?"

Tony squirmed a little. His eyes started to tear up. "I think so."

Mr. Brunswick placed a hand on his shoulder. "You need to be more careful around Regina. Now you'd better go home. I'll see you tomorrow, and don't forget to bring in more of your drawings." He smiled. "They really are good."

When Tony arrived home, he told Mom about the picture he'd drawn.

She hugged him. "Didn't I tell you that you were artistic?"

"Mom, I want to start packing for the camping trip. We're leaving right after school on Friday."

"Oh, the camping trip." She frowned. "Tony, I've been thinking." She placed a casserole in the oven. "I'm not so sure that's a good idea."

"Mom, you said I could go."

"I know, but what if the weather changes? I talked to Mrs. Todd, the neighbor across the street. She told me about a father and son who went mountain camping in September. Then, a blizzard caught them by surprise. They became separated, and the son froze to death."

"Mom, it's not going to storm." Tony plunked himself down into a kitchen chair.

"How do you know that?"

Tony tapped his fingers on the table. "I just know."

"Oh, Tony." She wiped her hands on her apron.

"Mom, we'll be careful, and I won't go anywhere by myself. Jed's dad isn't going to let me freeze to death. Remember, he's a member of the Search and Rescue Team."

"Let's see what the weather is like."

"I'm going," Tony said. "No matter what you say."

She pointed her finger at him. "You watch your mouth, Tony, or you won't be going anywhere."

Tony gritted his teeth. He stomped to his room, slammed the door, and threw himself down on the bed. She couldn't change her mind, not now. It wasn't fair.

After a while, Tony sat up and listened to some music on his iPhone. He looked around his blue and white bedroom. At least he was happy with his new room. The corner window had white curtains and looked out on an old apple tree covered with ripening apples. He could almost taste them. Tony smiled and began to hum along to the music. There was plenty of room for his double bed, dresser, and small desk. He liked the print of the clipper ship hanging above his dresser. Tony picked up his little model of a clipper ship and pretended it was riding the ocean waves. On a corkboard above his desk, he kept pictures of cats, horses, some of his drawings, and a cat calendar that Nana had given him.

Tony went out in to the kitchen. He leaned against the kitchen counter. Mom was washing some lettuce in the sink. She looked up at him, smiled, but didn't say anything. Mom had a local radio station on that was playing "oldies but goodies" music. He waited to hear a weather report. The late afternoon sun shone brightly through the window. In fact, the sun seemed to shine all the time in Wyoming, except for the day of the family picnic. Surely, the weather would be good for camping this weekend.

"Hope you're enjoying the weather as another day of the summer of 2017 slips away," the radio announcer cheerfully said. "Our downtown temperature is 78 degrees under clear skies."

Tony turned up the volume. "There's a possibility of a cold front in our long-range forecast, so we'll be keeping an eye on that."

Mom gave him that "all knowing" look.

Great. A possibility of a cold front meant an almost certain death to his camping trip, but maybe that was best. Then, he wouldn't have to worry about being attacked by a bear or struck by lightning.

Wait a minute. He could take care of himself. Why was he starting to think like his mom?

Guts

Late Friday afternoon, Tony couldn't believe he was standing by the edge of a placid blue lake.

"I'm glad the weather stayed warm," Jed said. He fastened his lifejacket.

"Me, too. I didn't think my mom was going to let me go." Tony grinned. "Did you see my mom's face when she saw the canoe on top of your dad's truck?"

"Yep. Didn't you tell her we were going canoeing?"

"I don't tell my mom anything unless I want a lecture on safety." Tony tried to fasten his lifejacket. The golden light of the late afternoon sun washed over him.

"Here, let me do that. I want to get out on the lake before it gets dark."

Mr. Logan watched as the boys prepared to launch the canoe. "Don't worry, Tony. Jed's been canoeing since he was five years old. He knows what he's doing, and I'll be watching you."

Tony wished he could be as confident as Jed.

"Where should I sit?" Tony fidgeted with his lifejacket. He'd never canoed before and was starting to doubt himself. What if he couldn't paddle?

"You sit up in the bow, that's the front of the canoe. I'll sit in the stern, the back, and steer." Jed slid the silver canoe into the still water and held it so Tony could get in. "Remember, don't stand up or you'll tip us over."

Jed didn't have to worry. Deep water, like so many things, frightened Tony. He'd be careful.

Jed pushed the canoe out on to the lake. Fish jumped, making dimples in the shiny surface. Far away mountain peaks shimmered in the soft light. The air smelled fishy. Tony swatted at a small swarm of gnats that crowded around his face.

"It's so peaceful." Tony dug his wooden paddle into the water with a splash, and it wiggled. The canoe swung abruptly to the right.

"Easy, Tony. You're going to make us go in circles," Jed said with a laugh. "Watch me."

Tony studied Jed's slow and steady movements with his paddle.

"Now, try it again."

Tony eased the paddle into the water and gently pushed it back. The paddle still wiggled, but not as much as the canoe pushed forward.

"That's better. You'll catch on."

Soon, he and Jed had the canoe gliding quietly across the lake.

"If we're quiet, we might see some wildlife. We'll stay close to the shore. Maybe we'll see an elk."

"Do you and your dad come here a lot?" Tony whispered.

"I guess. I'd like to come here more often, but ranching keeps Dad pretty busy."

"I wish my dad had a canoe." Tony stared at the forested shoreline.

"Tony, paddle closer to the side of the canoe. Like this." Jed gave the water a clean slice with his paddle.

"Sorry." Tony glanced back at Jed. "Do your arms ever get tired?"

"Are you tired already?" Jed grinned. "What a wimp."

"No. I just wondered." He really didn't want Jed to know how sore his arms were getting.

Tony and Jed canoed across the lake until the light faded and the lake's surface darkened. Swirls of coral sky reflected on the water. The canoe frightened a beaver. It slapped its tail and dove beneath the ripples.

"Jed, Jed, Jed," a voice echoed. "Supper, supper, supper."

"We'd better head back. Dad's calling," Jed said. "I'm starved."

Tony's stomach grumbled loud enough for Jed to hear. "Me, too."

Tony and Jed paddled toward Mr. Logan, who had been watching the boys while he prepared supper for them. He stood by the water's edge on the other side. Threads of blue-gray smoke filtered through the trees near the campsite. The world seemed to move in slow motion around him.

"You did pretty good once you got the knack of it, Tony."

"Thanks, Jed." Tony held his head a little higher. "I really like it."

The canoe had almost reached the shore when Tony noticed what looked like a large yellow dog. He pointed toward it.

"Is that a dog?" Tony asked.

"It's a bobcat."

"A bobcat!" Tony stood, without thinking, to get a better look.

"Sit down!" Jed shouted, but it was too late.

Tony lost his balance and flipped the canoe. He plunged into the icy water. Jed bobbed to the surface holding on to the canoe. Tony gasped as he found his footing in the waist high water.

"You turkey! I told you not to stand!" Jed smoothed back his wet hair. He grabbed the canoe.

"A little cold for a swim, boys." Jed's dad laughed.

"Funny, Dad." Jed splashed water at his dad and then broke into a smile and splashed Tony.

Tony splashed back and laughed.

"That's enough, boys," Mr. Logan said. "You'd better come in and dry off before you get hypothermia. I think Tony learned his lesson about standing up in a canoe."

Tony shivered and lowered his head. What if he had been in deep water?

He and Jed dried off and changed clothes. Then, they enjoyed a hot meal of beef stew and biscuits by the campfire. Tony ate two big bowls of the steamy stew. The fire crackled, giving off a warm glow that made Tony feel safe.

"You're a good cook, Mr. Logan." Tony poked at the fire with a long stick. "That's the best beef stew I've ever tasted."

"That wasn't beef, Tony," Jed said. "It was elk stew."

"Elk?" Tony's face scrunched up. "I've never had elk before."

"It tastes like beef." Jed stretched. "You couldn't even tell the difference. Dad's a good cook. He makes great stew, but his meatloaf is the worst." Jed gave his dad a playful punch in the arm.

"Come on, Jed. It's not that bad."

"Is your mom a good cook, too?" Tony asked.

"No!" Jed scowled and changed the subject without explaining.

Tony wondered why Jed became so angry when he had asked about his mom's cooking. Come to think of it, Jed never talked about his mom.

Jed picked up a package of marshmallows. "Let's toast some marshmallows. Have you ever toasted marshmallows before?"

"No, not really. Are they good?"

"Yep, try one."

Jed handed him a willow stick with a marshmallow poked onto the end. He told Tony to hold it over the hot coals and away from the flames. Tony held the marshmallow too close to the coals, and it burst into flames, burning it to a crisp. Jed showed Tony how to do it the second time. The gooey white liquid inside the golden-brown marshmallow cup tasted warm and sweet, so Tony toasted several more. He followed this treat with a cup of hot chocolate.

"Jed, I'm going to hit the sack. I'll see you in the morning. Be sure to put out the fire," Mr. Logan said, smoothing his red moustache. "Good night, Tony."

"Goodnight, Mr. Logan."

"Goodnight, Dad."

Tony watched Mr. Logan disappear into the tan tent. He sat, staring out on to the lake, on a log next to the campfire. Jed poked at the fire, sending a small shower of sparks glittering toward the night sky. Frantic flames danced as smoke spirals evaporated into the air. Tony liked the pungent smell of smoke. The heat from the fire burned into his face and hands, while the icy night tugged at his back. He was glad it was too cold for mosquitoes. Tony's thoughts settled on the flickering light of the campfire.

"Jed, do you ever get scared? I mean, like afraid you won't wake up or something?" Tony rubbed his hands together. He'd always wanted to share these thoughts with somebody, and he thought Jed might understand.

Jed thought for a moment. "You mean like dying?"

"Yeah."

"Sometimes."

"I remember when my grandpa died," Tony said. "I went into this big room filled with chairs and lots of flowers. Everyone was hugging and crying. Grandpa was in the coffin, and his face looked gray. He had a rosary wrapped around his hands like he was praying, but he never went to church. I touched his cold hand."

"You touched a dead person?" Jed grimaced.

"It was my grandpa."

"I didn't go to my grandmother's funeral." Jed scratched his head. "Dad said I was too small to go. I was only four when she died."

Tony stared deeper into the flames.

"I don't want to die like my brother, Joey. When you die, people don't care anymore. They bury you and try to forget about you."

"How did your brother die?"

"Some kind of accident. My nana told me. Mom and Dad don't talk about Joey, but I think that's why Mom worries so much about me."

Tony yawned and didn't say anything more.

Jed stood. "I'm ready for bed. You better use the outhouse, or you'll have to get up and go during the night."

"Right, and bears might be out." Tony held his hands over the fire. "Your dad told me he's never seen a bear in this campground."

"Black bear or grizzly?" Jed picked up an empty bucket. He walked toward the lake with his flashlight to get some water to put out the fire.

Tony waited by the fire. *Black bear or grizzly?* Jed must be trying to scare him. The night closed around him like a giant black plastic bag. He looked up at the moon shining just above the trees. The moon bulged full. Strange things happened on nights when the moon was full. The thought made him nervous.

After getting ready for bed, Tony snuggled deep into his sleeping bag. What would Mom say if she found out that he had tipped the canoe? This would probably be his last camping trip. He wondered if Jed's mom would react the same way. Mr. Logan was a nice guy, but what was Mrs. Logan like? And why wouldn't Jed talk about her? He rolled onto his side. The sleeping bag felt safe and warm. Tony closed his eyes and dreamed about hiking along the stream and fishing in the mountains.

The next morning, Tony heard the sound of the tent flap being unzipped by Mr. Logan.

"Rise and shine, boys. I want to get an early start up to Mirror Lake."

Tony slipped out of his sleeping bag and shivered in the cold air. He dressed as the smell of bacon wafted into the tent. Outside, light fog hovered above the lake.

"Ever had fresh trout?" Mr. Logan asked as he slid two fried eggs on to Tony's plate.

"Nope." Tony could see his breath.

"Nothing better than fresh trout." Mr. Logan took a sip of hot coffee. "We'll catch some for supper."

What if he messed up? Catching trout sounded like fun, but he didn't know how to fish. Mr. Logan had helped him get his fishing license at the Sports Lure before heading up the mountain and told him he could use their fishing poles. Tony gulped down his breakfast and prepared for the hike. Mr. Logan said it was about three miles to the lake.

At an altitude of about ten thousand feet, the thin air made it hard to breath. But the mountain scenery made Tony feel like he was on top of the world. It reminded him of a National Geographic documentary about the Rocky Mountains he had seen on TV. Snow glazed the peaks and the breeze chased itself among the pine and spruce spires that towered above him. The sun's rays warmed his navy-blue jacket, while chipmunks chattered nearby.

Mr. Logan stopped at the base of a small waterfall. Tony sat on a log while Jed stepped behind a tree to relieve himself. Mossy boulders and ferns surrounded the waterfall. Tiny fingers of ice fringed the shadowed edges of rock. Ribbons of water weaved among the rocks. Tony felt thirsty and bent over to get a drink.

"Tony, don't!" Mr. Logan shook his head.

"Why not?"

"I know the water looks clean, but you could get real sick from drinking it. The cattle dump in it, and you could get Giardia."

"What's Giardia?"

"It's a kind of bacteria that gets into your intestines," Mr. Logan said. "It gives you terrible cramps and diarrhea that can dehydrate you. If you're really thirsty, take a drink from my canteen instead."

Tony shrugged. "I guess I'd better. Thank you." Danger hid in unsuspecting places. He needed to learn how to take better care of himself.

The trail continued to wind through another meadow and then up to Mirror Lake. A cool breeze off the lake brushed Tony's face, which felt good after hiking uphill. Tony saw a large fish swimming near the shore.

"That's a trout," Jed said.

It was a lot bigger than Tony had thought. "Could I catch something that big?"

"Sure, it's easy. I'll show you."

Tony followed Jed over to a granite boulder. Jed took a fancy lure out of his tackle box and with Tony's help attached it to his fishing line.

"Now, watch me," Jed said.

Tony studied how Jed cast the fishing line. He made it look easy. When Tony tried it with his fishing pole, the lure caught in a pine tree behind him.

"Oops." Tony tried to pull the line free. "I don't think I can do it."

"Wait a minute. I'll get it," Jed said, walking over to the tree to untangle the lure. He gave Tony a reassuring smile as he walked back. "You can do it. I know you can."

Tony tried again and again, but he got his line tangled or his lure caught on shore every time.

"You're casting it out too hard. Go easy like this." Jed made another perfect cast.

Tony tried again, this time with less force, and the lure went far out into the lake. "Yes, I did it!"

Jed's grin spread ear to ear. "I knew you could do it."

After several more tries, Tony was casting like a pro.

"Remember, reel it in slowly," Jed said. "If you get a bite, jerk the line, but not too hard. Then, reel it in fast and steady."

"How will I know if I get a bite?" Tony asked.

"Oh, you'll know."

Tony continued to cast the fishing line and slowly reel it back in, but nothing happened. He watched several large trout pass by. Tony fished for what seemed like hours and didn't get a bite, while Jed caught two trout and Mr. Logan caught three.

"I told you I wouldn't catch anything." Tony scowled. "I can't... Whoa! Wait a minute. I've got a bite!"

Jed rushed over. "Give your line a jerk."

Tony jerked the line and began to reel something in. Whatever was on the other end pulled hard. He tried to steady the pole. Suddenly, he saw the glint of silver scales on the end of his line. The pole bent under the weight. He reeled and reeled until he jerked a large trout out of the water. It landed with a thud on the ground next to him, flipping and flopping.

"I got it! I got it!" Tony's eyes opened wide with excitement.

"All right, Tony," Jed said. "I knew you could do it."

"Good job," Mr. Logan said, slapping Tony on the back with his weathered hand. "We'll have fresh trout tonight."

Tony couldn't believe it. He'd caught a fish, a big fish. He couldn't wait to tell Dad.

"We'd better clean the fish and head back to camp," Mr. Logan said.

"Come on, Tony. I'll show you how to gut it," Jed said.

"Gut it?"

"Yep, you can't eat it if you don't gut it."

Jed removed a sharp knife from its sheath that was attached to his belt. He slit the bottom of the fish open and pulled out the blood-slimed guts. Tony could feel the bacon and eggs he'd had for breakfast jump to his throat. He ran behind a clump of willow bushes and vomited.

"Lose your cookies?" Jed said when Tony returned. He grabbed another fish to clean.

"Sorry." Tony wiped his mouth with the back of his hand. His shoulders slumped, and he hung his head down and looked at the ground. "I guess I'm not a real fisherman.

"You'll get used to it."

"I don't think so." Tony walked over to some rocks along the edge of the lake. He sat down on a boulder and thought. Why couldn't he be more like Jed? He felt foolish throwing up over a fish, but he couldn't help it. Regina could probably gut a fish with her teeth. How could he eat supper tonight without picturing those disgusting guts?

When it was time for supper, Tony decided he had to try the trout. He didn't want to offend Mr. Logan after he'd done so much to make this camping trip happen. Jed said his dad had cooked the trout to perfection. And after hiking most of the afternoon, Tony was hungry. Tony stared at the fish and slowly picked at it with his fork. He hesitated for a moment before he put a small piece into his mouth. To his surprise, the trout tasted delicious, and he ate his fill. Maybe he could be a real fisherman.

The next morning, Tony looked longingly out over the lake. He didn't want the trip to be over so soon. Tony helped Mr. Logan pack. Jed came up behind Tony and poked him in the side. Tony jumped like a startled cat.

"Why are you so jumpy? Did you think I was a bear?"

"Very funny." Tony picked up a camp chair and placed it into the truck.

"Do you want to go camping again sometime?" Jed asked.

"Do you mean it?" Tony wiped his hands on his jeans. "Even after I dumped the canoe and everything?"

"Sure. You're funny." Jed playfully punched Tony in the arm. "Besides, I want to see what you do when you see a real bear."

Tony grinned.

"Hey, I got an idea. Why don't you spend a weekend with me at the ranch?"

"Really? That'd be great."

"Maybe you could help butcher chickens." Jed laughed. "I'll even invite Regina."

Tony shoved Jed off balance.

"Just kidding."

The idea of spending a weekend at the ranch sounded great. He could ride a horse and pretend to be a real cowboy. Only… what if he couldn't ride a horse? What if he fell off and broke an arm or a leg? What if he saw a rattlesnake or a coyote? Maybe it wasn't such a good idea. Would Jed think he was so funny after a weekend at the ranch?

Pea-Green Manure

"Why not?" Tony asked Mom.

Mom scraped something off the kitchen counter with her fingernail. "I told you why."

"But Jed's dad said it was all right."

"I know, but you don't need to spend every weekend with Jed."

"Mom, come on. It's been two weeks since I went camping." Tony bit his lower lip.

"I said no. Now please take out the trash. I want to get rid of all the junk in the garage."

"But, Mom. I've never been to a ranch and…"

"I said NO!"

Tony kicked the leg of the kitchen chair and stomped to the garage. When he returned, his mom stood at the sink, peeling potatoes.

"I'm making fried potatoes," she said softly.

Tony didn't say anything.

"Don't be mad, Tony."

"Why not?" Tony slumped into the wooden chair.

"Tony, you don't understand." Mom wiped her forehead with the back of her hand.

"You always say that, Mom. What's to understand?" Tony poked at the floor with the tip of his shoe. "All I want to do is spend the weekend at Jed's."

"Tony, I don't want to argue."

"Well, it's not fair." Tony flicked a pencil across the table.

"A lot of things in life aren't fair."

"You never let me do anything because of Joey."

Mom slowly set the potato peeler down on the counter and wiped her hands on her apron. She turned toward Tony. "Tony, please."

"Why won't you talk about him? I had a brother, and I don't know anything about him."

Mom frowned and clasped her hands tightly. "Tony, don't."

"Why can't you tell me?" Tony felt a little bad as he saw tears well up in Mom's eyes.

"I can't talk about it. I just can't." She placed her hand over her mouth, burst into tears, and ran to her bedroom.

Tony clenched his teeth and pounded the table with his fist. He didn't mean to upset his mom, but it wasn't fair. Joey interfered with his life, and he wanted to know why.

That night, Tony didn't eat much at supper. Dad asked Tony if he was feeling okay. Tony simply told him he was tired, and Mom didn't question him. He did his homework and went to bed early. Darkness surrounded him, but he couldn't fall asleep. The bedroom door opened, and Dad peeked in.

"Tony, are you awake?"

"Yeah, I can't sleep."

Dad sat down on the edge of the bed next to him.

"Tony, I want you to listen carefully. Your mom just told me what happened today. I know you didn't mean to upset her."

"I didn't, Dad, but…"

"Please, just listen." He pushed the hair away from Tony's eyes. "Some things are better left alone. Do you know what I mean?"

"You mean Joey."

"Yes."

Tony looked at his dad's shadowed face in the light of the half-opened door. He looked tired and sad. What happened to Joey must have been terrible. Tony decided that for tonight he would let it go. He didn't want to upset his dad, too. Dad bent over and kissed him on the forehead.

"Goodnight, Tony."

"Dad?"

"What?"

"Could you talk to Mom about me going to Jed's ranch? Please."

"I'll talk with her. Now try to go to sleep."

Tony rolled over onto his side. "Thanks, Dad." Things looked better as he drifted off to sleep.

The rest of the week Tony could hardly keep his mind on his work. During class, he drew pictures on scratch paper of what Jed's horse, Hank, might look like and daydreamed about riding a horse with Jed. He fidgeted at home. All he could think about was going to the ranch. Would Jed's ranch be like what he'd seen on TV? Would he have to eat chicken?

Tony went out to Jed's ranch on Friday after school.

"I'm really glad your dad talked to your mom," Jed said, getting out of his father's truck. "We're going to have a great weekend!"

"Me, too," Tony said, following behind him. "Is that Hank over by the barn?"

"Yep, that's my horse. Come over and meet him."

"I'll take your bag in, Tony," Mr. Logan said. "Supper should be ready in a little while."

Tony and Jed walked over to the corral. Jed's chestnut gelding stood, swatting flies with his tail. The smell of horse manure was strong. To his surprise, Tony liked it. Jed called to Hank. The horse snorted and ambled over.

"Go ahead and pet him. He won't hurt you." Jed rubbed Hank's neck. "You're a pretty boy."

Tony hesitated and then stretched a hand toward the horse. Hank leaned forward to sniff it. Tony jerked back.

"He won't bite you. Let him sniff your hand."

Tony held out his hand again. The horse sniffed it. Feeling braver, Tony ran his hand along Hank's velvety neck. "Hi, Hank."

"See, I told you Hank's a good fellow." Jed rubbed the end of Hank's nose with the back of his hand. "I'll let you ride him tomorrow."

Tony gaped. "Me? Ride him? But I've never ridden a horse before."

"So you'll learn." Jed grinned. "Come on, let's go eat. I'm starved."

As Tony and Jed headed toward the ranch house, somebody tall and lanky, wearing jeans and a sweatshirt, limped onto the porch.

"Who's that guy?"

"That guy is my Aunt Billie."

Tony blushed. "Your aunt?"

"I know. She looks like a guy," Jed said. "Come on, I'll introduce you. She's my dad's sister."

Tony and Jed walked up to the porch. Billie waited with a wide grin and her hands on her hips. She was definitely not a guy. Tony noticed that she was wearing tiny turquoise earrings.

"Billie, this is Tony."

"Hi, Billie." Tony smiled.

She looked him over from top to bottom. "So, you're the greenhorn Jed's been talking about. Welcome," she said in a strong woman's voice. Billie shook Tony's hand firmly. "Come on in. Supper's ready. Looks like you could use something to eat."

At the dinner table, Tony tried not to stare at Billie as she sat down. She wore her thin gray hair cut short like a man's, and wire glasses slid down her nose. Tony studied the table set with baked beans, buttered carrots, a platter of fresh corn on the cob, a pitcher of dark brown gravy, chokecherry jelly, honey, and a large platter of fried chicken. Fried chicken. He remembered Jed's description of how they butchered the chickens, and a lump stuck in his throat. How was he going to eat that chicken?

Billie bowed her head and clasped her hands. "Let's say grace. Lord, bless this food which you have provided us. We thank you for your loving care and bless our new friend Tony. Amen. Now, eat up." Billie began passing the food with her large weathered hands. "There's plenty."

A big bowl of mashed potatoes steamed in front of Tony. The smell of fresh baked rolls made his mouth water. Tony wondered where Jed's mom was, but he didn't say anything.

"Jed says you ain't never rode a horse before." Billie piled a mound of mashed potatoes on her plate. "Nothing to it. Started ridin' when I was two. Rode all the time before I fell off old Nellie and broke my hip. Dumb horse reared over a rattlesnake."

Mr. Logan passed Tony the plate of chicken. "Come on, dig in. Raised it right here on the ranch."

"I know." Tony swallowed hard. "I'll start with just a small piece."

Jed glanced at Tony and chuckled.

"What's so funny?" Mr. Logan asked.

"Oh, nothing," Jed said, salting his potatoes.

Tony ate everything around the chicken first. Then, he poked at the chicken on his plate with the fork. In his mind, he could imagine the chicken flopping around with its head cut off.

"You always eat like that?" Billie asked.

"No." Tony fidgeted in his chair.

"Pick it up and eat it with your fingers." Billie shook her head. "Never did understand fancy manners and all."

Tony picked up the chicken leg. He closed his eyes and tried not to think about where it came from. It smelled good. He took a nibble.

"Billie makes the best fried chicken in the whole county. Right, Dad?"

"You bet."

"Flattery won't get you out of doing your chores, Jedidiah Logan," Billie said. "Tony can help you. Ever slopped hogs before?"

"No."

"Well, you'll get your chance tonight." Billie passed the platter of chicken. "Come on, boy. Eat up. I baked a fresh apple pie for dessert."

Tony took a bigger bite of the chicken. It was delicious. He felt relieved that he could eat the chicken without it coming back up on him, so he finished the leg and then had another piece.

After supper, Tony helped Jed with his chores. He watered and fed the horses. Then, he helped unload some fence posts from the back of the pickup truck. When the time came to slop the hogs, Jed let Tony pour the bucket of kitchen scraps into the pig trough. The hogs snorted and grunted, pushing their snouts deep into the slop. *Disgusting, but funny*, Tony thought.

"Now you know what it means to eat like a pig," Jed said.

"That big spotted one eats like Regina." Tony laughed.

Jed slapped Tony on the back. "No, it's got better manners."

Just before bed, Jed told Tony to follow him outside.

"Where are we going?" Tony asked.

"Up on the roof."

"What's up there? It's dark."

"Just follow me and be careful. I don't want you to fall and break something and spoil my weekend." Jed chuckled.

On the rooftop, Jed placed his hands behind his head and lay down.

Tony did the same. The shingles felt cool and scratchy on his back. He gazed up into the night sky.

"Holy cow! I've never seen so many stars," Tony said. "Back in New York you couldn't see many stars at night. Too many lights." Tony breathed deeply. The scent of sagebrush and the stars twinkling above made him feel peaceful.

Jed pointed. "See the Big Dipper?"

"Yep. Is that the Milky Way?"

"Sure is. Amazing, isn't it?"

"I've only seen pictures of it. Wow! This is unbelievable." Tony lost himself in the universe before him. Was Joey looking down on him? Tony suddenly felt very small. A soft cool breeze drifted over them. Jed and Tony settled into quiet thoughts and studied the sky for a long time.

Jed broke the silence after a while. "Billie calls it *God's Masterpiece in the Sky.*"

Tony couldn't agree more. A shooting star dashed across the sky, and Tony lifted his head.

"Holy cow! I've never seen a shooting star."

"I see them all the time."

"Do you come up here a lot?"

"Sure. Sometimes with my dad."

"My mom would never let me. She'd be afraid I'd fall off the roof and break a leg or something."

Jed laughed. "We'd better climb down and get to bed. Tomorrow, we'll have to get up early. Billie doesn't let anyone sleep in."

The next morning, after an enormous breakfast of scrambled eggs, toast, bacon, and fresh blueberry muffins, Jed helped Tony get ready for his first horse ride.

"You always get up on the left side of the horse," Jed said as he steadied the horse and handed the reins to Tony. "Take the reins and hold onto the saddle horn. Now put your left foot into the stirrup and lift your right leg over the saddle and onto the right side of the horse. See how easy that was?"

As Tony sat in the saddle on top of Hank, he wondered if he could really do this without getting hurt. Hank seemed gentle, but what if the horse spooked? He could end up limping like Aunt Billie. After the canoe incident, Tony definitely didn't want to mess this up, too. His stomach felt like it was filled with miller moths.

"You look good in my old cowboy hat. I think you should keep it," Jed said. He started out of the corral on a blue roan named Tibbs. He looked back at Tony. "Just relax and think about what I told you. Remember, to turn Hank, you pull the reins gently to the left or right. Give him a little nudge with your heel to make him go. To stop him, pull the reins back, but not too hard. Hank's pretty easy to handle."

Tony nudged Hank with his heel and followed Jed out of the corral. So far, riding a horse seemed easy. Tony and Jed walked the horses to the pasture behind the dark, weathered, wooden barn.

"Are all those black cows over there yours?" Tony said.

"Yep. They're Black Angus, beef cattle."

"Do they all fit in this barn?"

Jed laughed. "No. We don't keep cattle in the barn."

"Not even in winter?"

"Nope. The cattle stay out all winter, and we feed them hay in the fields."

Tony shrugged his shoulders. "In New York, the barns are painted red, and the cows stay in the barns in winter."

"I guess Wyoming cattle are tougher." Jed laughed.

In the distance, Tony could see pumpkin-colored buttes and frosted mountain peaks. The sun's rays warmed the back of his neck. A black raven cawed on a fencepost. He could hear the steady clop, clop, clop of the horse's hooves on the dusty road, and he felt like a real cowboy.

"Tony, let's go over there." Jed pointed toward some juniper-covered hills. "Give Hank a little kick and make a clicking sound like me. He'll speed up for you. Hold on."

Tony frowned. "I don't want to hurt him."

"I didn't say wallop him. Just give him a little kick. He's used to it."

Tony tapped the horse's flank very lightly with his heels, and Hank began to trot. Tony bounced in his saddle. The longer he rode, the more in tune with the rhythm of the horse he became. He could ride! Tony and Jed rode higher into the sparsely covered hills, and the barn disappeared from sight. He saw several rabbits hopping among the sagebrush. Then, Tony spied a flash of red.

"Jed, look over there by that dead tree. What's that?"

"Looks like a fox. Let's ride over and get a closer look."

Tony followed Jed. As he approached the dead tree, he again spotted the reddish-brown fox running along the rim of rocks. Jed stopped at the top of the ridge, and Tony watched the fox disappear into the sagebrush. "This is great," Tony said. "I've never seen a fox in the wild."

"Last spring, I saw a mother fox playing with her four pups. They're a lot like dogs."

Tony pet Hank's neck. "I wish I could've seen that. One of my neighbor's dogs had puppies once. It was fun to watch them wrestle with each other."

"Let's head over to the stock tank and water the horses," Jed said.

Tony and Jed dismounted and let the horses drink. Tony thought he heard a chattering sound coming from a large clump of sagebrush near the tank. "What's making that sound?" Tony said. He stepped over to get a closer look.

"Don't move, Tony! Rattler!"

Tony sucked in a big breath and froze as Jed picked up a shovel resting by the side of the tank. His friend moved quickly toward the clump and raised the shovel high into the air. Then, with all his might, he brought the shovel down on the snake, slicing its head off. The snake's head fell to the side, still opening and closing its mouth. There was hardly any blood, but the body began violently flopping all around. Tony jumped farther away from the writhing serpent.

"Why is it still moving? I thought you killed it."

"I did, but a rattlesnake's metabolism is very slow. Its organs don't die as fast, so they can keep moving." Jed placed the shovel back next to the tank.

"One time, I heard a snake head bit somebody ninety minutes after it was decapitated."

Tony shivered. "That's gross." He grimaced and exhaled like a balloon deflating. "You just saved my life!"

Jed shrugged. "Not really, you weren't close enough to get bitten."

Tony stared at the snake and back to Jed. "But…" Tony felt himself shaking and breathing fast.

"You all right?" Jed asked.

Tony nodded. "That was a close call. You did save my life."

Jed shrugged his shoulders and smiled. "Okay, if you say so." After waiting for several minutes for the snake to stop moving, he took out a pocket knife and cut off the snake's rattler. He handed it to Tony. "Here, keep this as a souvenir."

"Wow! A real rattle from a snake." Tony placed it in his shirt pocket. "Thanks."

"Better not show your mom, or she might freak out and never let you come back here to visit," Jed said, mounting his horse. "Come on, let's ride."

Tony and Jed followed the fence line of the Logan Ranch for about an hour and then started home.

Jed broke the silence as they got closer to the ranch house. "Make sure you hold on to Hank now."

"Why?"

"He knows when he's headed back to the barn and sometimes he gets a little excited."

"Oh, I'm all right. Hank and I are friends," Tony said. He patted the horse's neck.

When Hank saw the barn, his nostrils flared. He raised his head, snorted, and took off like a rocket.

"Whoa! Whoa! Whoa!" Tony shouted. He pulled on the reins, but Hank raced toward the barn, and Tony bounced like a rag doll. Fear pulled at his insides as the horse charged ahead. Jed followed close behind, but he couldn't stop Hank. Tony held on tight. He no longer had control of his new friend. His fears about breaking a limb came rushing back. He felt scared and excited at the same time. The miller moths had found their way back into his stomach, and beads of sweat erupted on his forehead. His hat flew off, but he had to hold on to the reins.

Tony managed to stay on Hank until the horse rushed into the barnyard. Hank came to an abrupt halt, flinging Tony into a pile of steaming, pea-green manure. The thud knocked the wind out of him.

"Are you okay?" Jed asked, getting down off his horse.

Tony sat, stunned.

"Tony, you okay?"

He took a deep breath and stood. "I think so." Then, he realized that manure covered his hands and backside. "Gross! I'm covered with…"

"I know," Jed said, laughing. "You're covered with horse poop. Fresh horse poop."

"Yuck!" Tony tried to shake the green crud from his hands.

"Better get you cleaned up." Billie grinned from ear to ear as she looked down at Tony. Where had she come from?

"I saw you drop in from the kitchen window. Thought I'd better make sure you was all right." She placed her hands on her hips. "Looks like nothin's been hurt, 'cept maybe your pride."

Tony nodded. "I didn't get hurt, but this is gross." Tony held out his hands and grimaced.

"Sure is." Billie laughed from deep down in her belly.

Jed laughed, too. "Wish I had a camera. If only your mom could see you now. She'd probably disinfect you right on the spot."

Then, Tony realized how funny he must look and started to laugh, too.

"Thanks, Hank," Tony said sarcastically. "We'll have to do this again sometime."

"You go get cleaned up, and I'll go get your hat," Jed said, turning Tibbs around.

After Billie helped Tony get cleaned up, he and Jed climbed up to the hayloft. Jed wanted to show Tony where the barn cats stayed. Tony sat down on a bale of hay, and Jed sat next to him. The hay smelled sweet.

Tony hesitated for a moment. "We're good friends now, aren't we, Jed?"

"Sure. I let you ride my horse, didn't I?" Jed chuckled.

Tony smiled. "Then, would you tell me something?"

"What?"

"Where's your mom?"

Tony could see Jed's face turn as red as his hair and tighten. He stood and kicked a bale of hay.

Tony wasn't expecting Jed to get angry. "What's wrong?"

"What's wrong is that she walked out, just packed her bags and left."

Tony didn't know what to say. Jed kicked the bale of hay again.

"I HATE her! She never even said goodbye."

Tony had never seen Jed act this way before. He wished he hadn't asked. "I'm sorry. I didn't mean to make you mad."

"I knew you'd ask, but I don't want to talk about it. Let's go see if Billie's cookies are done."

Tony followed Jed down the ladder and out of the barn. Maybe having an overprotective mom was better than having a mom that didn't care.

Sweet Perfume

HONK HONK HONK!

"What was that?" Tony jumped out of his warm bed and raced to the slightly open corner window. He looked to the sky and saw a large V-formation of geese. The geese were flying south for the winter.

Tony ran to the kitchen where his mom and dad stared out the window.

"Good morning, Tony," Mom said.

"Did you hear the honking?" Dad took a sip of coffee.

"Yep. Let's go outside and see them."

"Sure. Grab a jacket. It's chilly out this morning," Dad said. "Come on, Frances. I've always wanted to see the geese flying south."

Tony and his parents went out to the backyard to watch the geese. The squawking flock flew overhead.

"We're watching one of nature's wonders." Dad hugged Mom. "Isn't it fascinating, Frances?"

"It's wonderful." Mom snuggled up to Dad.

Plop. A large white glob appeared on Mom's shoulder. She touched it with her finger. "Gene, is that what I think it is?" She gasped. "It's bird poop, isn't it?"

"I think so." Dad tried to cover up a smile with his hand.

"Oh, how disgusting!" Mom said. "I'm going inside."

Tony and his dad burst into laughter as Mom stomped into the house.

"Well, that certainly ruined a special moment," Dad said.

"I don't think Mom will forget this." Tony placed his hand on Dad's shoulder and glanced back up to the geese honking their way south.

After breakfast, Tony left for school. He couldn't wait to tell Jed what had happened.

Regina greeted him at the entrance to the school playground.

"Hi, Tony." Regina snapped her gum and smiled. She held something in her hand. "Want some chocolate?"

"No, thanks." Tony pushed the hair back from his eyes.

"What's the matter? Don't you like chocolate?" She twisted the ends of her long blond hair with her hand.

Tony hesitated and then held out his hand. Maybe she was just trying to be nice.

"Okay." Tony took the candy and looked at it. "Are you sure this is candy?"

Regina smiled the biggest smile he'd ever seen from her. "Yep, my mom only lets me have it once in a while. It's special dark chocolate."

Tony took a small nibble of the chocolate. "Gee, thanks." The chocolate was kind of bitter, but it wasn't bad. He popped the rest of it into his mouth.

"Hey, Tony," Jed called from across the playground.

"I'd better go." Tony smiled at Regina and walked over to Jed.

"How's it going?" Jed asked.

"Great!"

"What's up with Regina?"

"Oh, she's just being nice for a change."

"Regina, nice?" Jed asked. "You must be joking. She's a rattler just waiting to strike."

Tony told Jed about the geese dropping a surprise on his mom's shoulder. Jed laughed and told Tony about the time a magpie pooped on his burger at a picnic. Tony thought that was really gross.

When Tony entered the classroom, Regina gave him a big smile, and a couple of her friends waved at him and began to giggle. What was going on?

"Class, today I'd like to talk to you about the Halloween Window Painting Contest being held by the Chamber of Commerce. Several of the stores in town will have students paint Halloween scenes on the inside of their store front windows for the holiday. There will be a first, second, and third place prize for the best window painting."

Tony and Jed looked at each other. Maybe he could enter the contest and win a prize. It might be fun. Mr. Brunswick explained the rules and handed out the entry forms. Tony listened closely.

"I hope some of you will enter. You might win." Mr. Brunswick looked directly at Tony.

Did Mr. Brunswick think he could win? He would try.

Tony's stomach began to feel nauseous, like the inside of a washing machine. It started to gurgle and rumble. He placed his hands over his stomach. He scrunched up his face, raised his hand, and blurted out, "Mr. Brunswick, may I please go to the restroom?"

Mr. Brunswick looked surprised and nodded. Tony raced out to the restroom to the sound of muffled giggles. He had major diarrhea and almost didn't make it to the restroom in time. What had made him so sick? Then, it dawned on him. It must have been Regina's special chocolate.

The morning passed slowly. He had to be excused to go to the restroom two more times before recess. He didn't feel very good, but, for a change, Tony understood the math lesson on multiplying fractions. Math didn't come easy for him. He liked reading and writing better and art most of all. Tony noticed Regina and her friends watching him. He fidgeted in his chair. They must have known what she had done.

At recess, Regina seemed to be following him around.

"What's with Regina?" Jed asked Tony. "She sure seems interested in you today." Jed leaned on the brick wall of the school. "Maybe she's got a crush on you."

Tony looked away. He didn't want to tell Jed about the chocolate. "I don't think so. Maybe she likes you."

Jed laughed. "Forget it. I'd rather have an old sow for a girlfriend."

"Hey, Tony. Come here," Regina yelled, hiding something behind her back. "I want to show you something."

"You'd better watch her," Jed said.

Tony tried to ignore her, but she kept calling to him and started walking his way.

"Come here. Don't you want to see what I have?"

Tony turned and hurried toward the school building. Regina chased after him.

She held up a small pink water balloon. "Catch!" Regina threw the balloon at Tony.

He raised his hands by instinct and was surprised when the balloon flew right to them. It burst and spattered all over him. Suddenly, he smelled like his Aunt Mary. The balloon must have been filled with some cheap perfume.

"I knew it," Jed said, lowering the hands that had been protecting his face. "She got you good. What's that awful smell?"

"Guess. Achoo!" Tony sneezed. He wiped his hands on his jeans as the bell rang.

Inside the classroom, Tony sat down next to Regina. He sneezed and gave her a dirty look. She grinned at him. Some of the other kids began pinching their noses and waving their hands. He wished Regina would move to another country. Tony sneezed again.

"Bless you, Tony," Mr. Brunswick said, walking toward the blackboard. "Class, take out your spelling books. Today, we're going to—phew! Which one of you girls put on the perfume?"

"It's not a girl," one of Regina's friends blurted out. "It's Tony."

Tony sneezed again. His eyes began to water, and his eyes felt itchy. Tears rolled down his face, but he wasn't crying. He sneezed repeatedly.

"Tony, what's the matter? You've been to the restroom a lot today, and now your eyes look puffy." Mr. Brunswick picked up his pointer stick. "You'd better go see the nurse."

The nurse figured Tony was allergic to the perfume and decided to send him home. All the girls giggled as Tony grabbed his jacket to leave. He sneezed all the way home. His eyes watered so much he could hardly see his mom when she met him at the door.

"Tony, the nurse called me." She lifted his chin and looked into his eyes. "Are you all right? You look pale. How did you get perfume all over you? You smell like your Aunt Mary."

"Mom, I feel miserable." Tony rubbed his eyes and sneezed.

"Let's get you into the shower. The nurse thinks you'll be fine after a shower, some clean clothes, and a dose of this allergy medicine."

After showering, Tony did feel much better. He sat down to watch some TV with Mom and have lunch.

"So, how did you get covered with perfume?" Mom asked again, handing Tony a sandwich plate and a glass of milk.

"Some girl threw a balloon filled with perfume at me." Tony picked up his sandwich. "I caught it, but the balloon burst in my hands."

"Was it that girl who's always bothering you?" Mom asked, handing him a napkin. "That Gina?"

"Her name's Regina."

"Regina should be taught a lesson," Mom said angrily shaking her finger at him. "Your allergic reaction could have been worse. You could have stopped breathing."

"Oh, Mom. Stop exaggerating."

"Well, I'm going to call her mother and let her know what she did to you."

"Mom, please don't." Tony scowled. "I can take care of myself."

Mom took a stance and placed her hands on her hips. "I'm sorry, Tony, but I've made up my mind."

"Mom!"

Tony felt lucky when Regina's mother didn't answer the phone. Later that day, he overheard his parents talking about what had happened.

"Gene, that girl should be punished! Tossing a perfume balloon isn't funny. I can't believe a young girl could be so mean," Mom said.

"Calm down, Frances. It was just a joke that backfired. You can't butt into Tony's business or you'll make matters worse. He has to learn to take care of himself, or he'll never grow up."

"Take care of himself! Why just look at what happened today. He can't take care of himself. He needs me."

"Frances, be reasonable."

"No, I'm going to call her mother again. She should be home by now. I'll let her know what kind of a brat she's raising."

Tony heard his mom stomp off toward the kitchen phone. His stomach flipped. What a mess. Maybe Mom was right. Maybe he couldn't take care of himself.

When Tony arrived at school the next day, he searched the playground for Regina, but there was no sign of her. He saw Jed and Randy playing on the monkey bars.

"Hey, guys. How's it going?" Tony asked.

"Great," Jed said swinging from the bar. "You smell any better today?"

"Funny." Tony kicked at the ground with his foot.

"I told you not to trust Regina. After you went home, she bragged about the perfume balloon. She was pretty proud of herself."

Tony felt the blood rush to his cheeks. He looked down.

"Hey, guys. Here comes the old sow now," Randy said.

Regina charged up to Tony. She could have been a football player with such broad shoulders. Regina shoved Tony. He fell backwards on to the asphalt.

"You big baby. Your mom called, and now I'm grounded for two weeks. Two weeks!" Regina raised her fists at him.

Tony stood up. "I-I-I didn't make my mom call." Tony rubbed his hands on his thighs.

"Oh, sure, you little wimp. I'm going to get you for this!" Regina stomped off.

Tony turned away. What could he say? The bell rang.

"Let's go, Tony," Jed said. "She's just full of hot air. Forget it."

Tony knew better. She'd get him.

Back in the classroom, Mr. Brunswick placed his hand on Tony's shoulder and asked him if he'd thought anymore about the painting contest. He suggested that Tony make some sketches for him to look at and offered him sketching paper.

Except for a little giggling from his classmates at the beginning of class, the rest of the day went well. After school, Regina left him alone, which made him nervous. He couldn't change the fact that Mom had called Regina's mother, so he turned his thoughts to the contest.

Tony noticed corn shocks—dried corn stalks tied up in bundles that Randy had told him about—in a neighbor's garden on his way home. Bright orange pumpkins lay scattered around the base of the shocks. Suddenly, he had an idea for the painting contest.

He ran the rest of the way home and rushed into the house.

"Tony, what's the big hurry?" Mom asked.

"I've got an idea for the Halloween Painting Contest. I want to get it down on paper."

"I think it's wonderful that you're entering the contest." She wrapped the cord around the vacuum cleaner. "You've always been my little artist."

"Mom, I'm not little." Tony pulled out some blank paper and a pencil from a kitchen drawer and sat down at the table.

"I know, but you're still my artist." Mom winked at him.

Tony rolled his eyes. Would Mom always think of him as a baby?

He began to sketch corn shocks with pumpkins all around. Then, he made an extra-large shock and left the center hollow. Inside the empty space, he drew a haunted house with ghosts and bats flying around it.

"Did Regina leave you alone today?" Mom washed her hands at the kitchen sink.

"Yes," Tony mumbled.

"You know, I think…"

"Mom, I don't want to talk about it." Tony set the pencil down.

"I know, dear, but …"

"Mom, you've already messed things up." Tony stood. "Just forget it." Tony wanted to forget about Regina and wished that she'd never been born.

The telephone rang, and Mom answered it.

"Tony, it's for you." Mom handed him the phone.

"Hello."

"Hi, Tony. It's Jed."

"What's up?"

"Well, Randy told me Regina said that you'd never win the painting contest. She'd make sure of it."

Tony didn't say anything. He nervously tapped his foot.

"Hey, Tony you still there?"

"Yep, I'm here."

"I think you'd better keep an eye on that old sow. You never know what she might do."

"Thanks, Jed. I gotta go. See you tomorrow."

Tony hung up the phone, and his stomach knotted. Regina wanted revenge, and she'd get it.

Surprises

On Saturday afternoon, Tony went to the Prescription Shop, the local pharmacy, to begin painting the contest window. Mr. Brunswick liked his idea about the corn shocks and had made some suggestions on how to improve it. Tony brought a box of tempera paints, brushes, rags, and his sketch of the painting. Excitement whirled in his stomach.

"I'll show Regina. I'm going to win this contest," he said to himself. But, in his heart, he wasn't so sure.

Tony painted the outline of the main corn shock on the inside of the window. The thin brown paint dripped down the window. He needed to mix in more powder. He wiped the excess paint off the window, glad that he had remembered the rags.

Tony painted, trying to remember everything his art teacher at his old school, Mr. Sanchez, had taught him. After about an hour, he heard a tapping on the window. Jed waved hello. Tony motioned him to come in.

"Hi, Jed."

"Tony, it's looking great." Jed studied the painting. "I wish I could paint like you."

Tony took a deep breath. "So, you think it's good?"

"Good? It's great!" Jed adjusted his cowboy hat. "I've seen some of the other windows and none of them look as good as yours."

Tony dabbed at the edge of a pumpkin that had begun to drip. "It'll probably take me most of the afternoon to finish."

"Well, I gotta go." Jed opened the door. "Aunt Billie made me a dentist appointment. Just a check-up."

"ZZZZZZZZZ!" Tony placed his hand on his jaw and grimaced. "Have fun."

"Right. See ya." Jed gave Tony a playful punch in the arm.

Tony worked carefully on the painting. He blended colors, highlighted, and used lots of detail. When he finished the window, he stepped outside and studied it. He took a deep breath and smiled. On Monday, the judges would select a winner, and maybe, just maybe, it would be him.

As he cleaned up, he heard another tap on the window. He glanced up to see Regina's scowling face. She opened her mouth wide, stuck out her tongue, and jabbed her pointer finger in like she was going to throw up. Tony turned away. Regina banged on the window again. This time, she waved a big X over the painting with her hands, like she was going to get rid of it. She laughed and entered the store.

"I've seen better paintings on bathroom walls," Regina said, placing her hands on her hips.

"Nobody asked you." Tony swirled a dirty paintbrush in a container of water as if to whisk her away.

"It doesn't matter. You aren't going to win anyway."

"How do you know?" Tony wiped the paintbrush dry with a rag.

Regina twisted the ends of her hair and marched out the door. "I know."

"What does she know?" Tony mumbled, wiping his hand on a wet rag.

"Did you say something?" Mr. Martin, the storeowner asked, popping up behind him.

"No. Just talking to myself."

"Was Regina bothering you?" Mr. Martin folded his arms.

"No more than usual."

"I guess she can really be annoying," Mr. Martin said. "Her mother cleans the store for me, and Regina hangs around sometimes. Never has anything nice to say."

Tony nodded his head in agreement.

"The window looks great, Tony. I hope you win."

"Thanks, Mr. Martin. I'll find out on Monday."

Tony gathered his materials and said goodbye. He decided to check out the other window paintings in town. Most of the paintings looked good, but he thought his painting might have a chance to win. Tony hurried home. He wanted to show his parents what he had done.

"Mom, I finished," Tony shouted as he entered the house. "Can you come and see it?"

"Tony, how many times have I asked you not to slam the door?" Mom said.

"Sorry." Tony grabbed an oatmeal cookie from the cookie jar. "Can you and Dad come see my painting? It's finished."

"Well, I was just going to start supper." Mom placed a pot of water on the stove. "But I guess it can wait a few minutes."

"Great! I'll call Dad."

Tony's dad parked in front of the Prescription Shop. Mom and Dad hopped out of the car to take a closer look. Tony held his breath, waiting for them to say something.

"You did a good job, Tony. I'm impressed," Dad said.

"Reminds me of autumn back East," Mom said. "I love the idea of having the haunted house in the middle of the hollowed-out pumpkin. Do you think you should have used a brighter orange for the pumpkin?"

"Oh, Mom." Tony shook his head.

"I wasn't being critical." Mom pointed to the pumpkin shell. "I just thought…"

Tony pushed his hands into his pockets. "I know, Mom, but it's too late anyway." This was no time for her to make suggestions.

Mom gave him a hug and Dad smiled. Tony could tell his parents liked the painting. He felt like a helium balloon ready to take flight. Now if he could just win the contest.

Later that evening, the phone rang, and Mom answered it. Tony figured it was long distance by the way Mom's face brightened.

"Who is it, Mom?" Tony said, trying to get her attention.

"It's Nana." She shooed him away with a wave of her hand. "I'll let you talk to her in a minute."

Tony could hardly wait. Over two months had passed since he'd said goodbye to Nana in New York. When Mom handed him the phone, he had so much to say he didn't know where to start.

"Hi, sweetheart," Nana said. "How are you?"

"Hi, Nana." Tony sat down on a stool by the kitchen counter. "I'm good. I have a new friend, and we camped in the mountains. I stayed at his ranch and rode a horse. And I've entered a painting contest."

"That's wonderful!" Nana said. "I miss you so much. I don't know why your parents had to move so far away."

"I miss you, too. I can't wait to see you again," Tony said.

"Tony, I have a big surprise for you. I'm going to spend Christmas with you."

"Really?" Tony hopped off the stool, his mouth open wide.

"Yes, I can hardly wait. I'll bake you some Italian cookies and make homemade sauce."

"Whaa hoo!" Tony shouted. "That's great, Nana!"

"You'd better let me talk to your mom now; we've got plans to make. I'll see you at Christmas. I love you."

"Bye, Nana. I love you, too." Tony handed the phone to his mom.

He couldn't believe it. Nana was going to spend Christmas with him in Wyoming. He'd have to think of a special gift for her. Maybe he could make a miniature of the window painting and have Dad help him frame it.

Things looked brighter all the time. He had a good chance at winning the contest, and now Nana was going to visit. What more could he ask for?

About a half hour later, Tony received a phone call from Jed.

"Hey, Tony," Jed said. "How would you like to go with dad and me up to Bozeman the second weekend of November? My dad's going to an auction."

"Sure. Sounds like fun." Tony tapped his foot excitedly. "Where's Bozeman?"

"It's in Montana. Ask your mom if you can go with us, if she's in a good mood."

"Oh, she's in a good mood." Tony tapped his fingers on the kitchen counter. "Nana called, and she's coming to spend Christmas with us."

"All right!" Jed gave a sigh of relief. "Go ahead and ask her."

"Hold on," Tony said. He turned toward his mom with pleading eyes. "Mom, could I go with Jed and his dad to Bozeman, Montana the second week of November? His dad's going to an auction."

"Isn't that the week of the community concert?" Mom asked. "Don't you want to go to the concert with me and Dad?"

"Not really."

"Well, I suppose." Mom picked a dead violet blossom off a plant in the kitchen window above the sink. "But you have to promise me that you'll wear your seatbelt."

"I promise," Tony said. "Jed, it's okay. I can go."

"Great! That was easy for a change. I'll let you know more about it later. See ya."

"See ya." Tony hung up the telephone.

"Tony, I have to pick up Nana at the airport on December 22nd. She's flying in to Sheridan about six thirty in the evening. Can you believe it?" Mom said, rolling up her sleeves. "My mother's flying out to see us."

"Has Nana ever flown before?"

"No. She's always been afraid to fly, but she misses us so much she doesn't care. I just hope the weather is good when she flies into Sheridan. I've heard horror stories about people traveling at holiday time."

"You worry too much, Mom."

Mom looked around the kitchen. "There's so much to do before she gets here. You'll have to help me."

Tony tapped his fingers on the kitchen table. Christmas was still over two months away. What could she possibly have to do that would take that much time?

"Let me guess." Tony pretended to look thoughtful. "Another major cleaning campaign?"

"Yes, a major cleaning campaign." Mom jokingly pointed a finger at him, "And you're going to help."

Tony saluted. "Yes, ma'am, sir."

Mom chuckled, and Tony grinned. What a great day!

The next morning, he overslept. Even though he was in a hurry because he didn't want to be late for school, he decided to take one last look at his painted window. Today, he felt sure that his painting would win.

As he came upon the Prescription Shop window, he gasped. No! It couldn't be. The painting had been smeared. It looked like somebody had taken a wet rag and dragged it over the window from the inside. Who could have done this? His eyes began to blur as a lump the size of a basketball filled his throat. He wasn't going to win any prize now.

Tony rushed off to school. Anger bubbled up inside him like boiling water. Somebody must really hate him. Regina. It had to be. But how? Then, he remembered her mother cleaned the store at night, and sometimes Regina hung around.

The tardy bell rang just as Tony opened the classroom door. Out of breath, he burst into the room and marched over to Regina. "You did it! Didn't you?"

"Did what?" Regina said, shaking her long curls.

Everyone quieted down and stared at Tony.

"What did I ever do to you? Why can't you leave me alone?" Tony shook with anger. "I could have won."

"What are you talking about?" Regina scowled.

"You know." Tony clenched his fists.

"You'd better shut up before I punch your face in." Regina glared at Tony.

Tony took a step closer. "Maybe you should try…"

"What's going on here?" Mr. Brunswick stepped between Tony and Regina. "I'm surprised at you, Tony."

"Yes, Tony. I'm surprised at you," Regina mimicked.

"That's enough, Regina," Mr. Brunswick said, frowning in disapproval at her. He turned to Tony. "What's wrong?"

Tony stared at Regina. He started to say something but stopped.

Mr. Brunswick placed his hand on Tony's shoulder. "I asked you what's wrong?"

"It doesn't matter. It's too late anyway." Tony's shoulders slumped, and he looked down at the floor.

Mr. Brunswick shook his head. "Then you'd better both sit down so I can start class."

Tony sat down. Strange how one person could mess up your life. He realized how much he had really wanted to win the contest. He wanted to be able to call Nana and tell her that he'd won a painting contest. She would have been so proud of him. It was too late now. What would he tell his parents?

Tony acted as if nothing had happened when he arrived home from school. Mom reminded him that he might get a "winning phone call," but Tony knew better.

"You're awfully quiet, Tony. Anxious about the contest?" Mom picked a piece of lint from his shirt.

Tony pulled away. "I guess."

"Tony, could I see you in the garage for a minute? I need your help," Dad said.

"Sure."

When Tony stepped into the garage, Dad placed his hand on his shoulder. "Do you want to talk about it?" Dad's face looked serious.

"About what?"

"I drove past the Prescription Shop after work."

Tony's feelings tumbled around in his head like clothes in a dryer. What could he say? He felt tears gathering at the corners of his eyes and furiously blinked them away.

"Dad, it's not fair." Tony kicked the door. "I never did anything to Regina, and she won't leave me alone. She's ruining my life."

"Life isn't always fair, son."

"You won't tell Mom, will you, Dad?" Tony pleaded.

"No. I won't say anything." Dad rubbed his chin. "You have to learn to solve your own problems."

Tony sighed in relief.

"So, what are you going to do?" Dad leaned back against the workbench.

"I don't know."

Tony heard the telephone ring from the kitchen window. He wished it was the contest judge, but it couldn't be.

Suddenly, a scream burst from inside the house. Tony followed Dad as he rushed into the house. Mom stood with her hand over her mouth. Tears trickled down her face. The telephone lay on the counter.

"Hello, hello ..." a voice said from the phone.

Just Like Joey

"No. It can't be," Tony whispered. "I just talked to her on Sunday."

"Nana was a spunky old lady," Dad said. "But a heart attack can happen to anyone."

"But why did it have to happen to Nana?" Tony's eyes teared up.

Dad folded his hands and leaned against the counter. "I don't know, Tony."

"Poor Mom." Tony sighed. "I've never seen her cry so hard."

"Mom's going to need our help to get through all this."

"Can I go into the bedroom to see her now?"

"I think that would be a good idea." Dad hugged Tony.

Tony walked down the hall to his parents' bedroom. Mom was lying on the bed, facing the window. Tony watched her for a moment before he spoke.

"Mom, I'm sorry. Are you all right?" Tony wiped his sweaty hands on his thighs.

She reached out her hand to him. "Mama's gone. My mama's gone."

Tony knelt down next to her and held her hand. Then, all the hurt his heart could no longer bear burst out into a torrent of tears. He'd never see her again. Nana wouldn't be coming for Christmas.

After Mom left for the funeral in New York, the house seemed empty. New York seemed farther away than ever. He wished he could have gone back, but money was a problem. For the next two weeks, he and Dad would be on their own.

Tony was afraid. What if she didn't come back? She could have a heart attack, or her plane could crash. What if he couldn't take care of himself? Tony tried to chase the worries out of his head. Right now, he had to get supper started for Dad. He planned to make something easy like eggs and toast. He'd made that before.

Tony set the table first, like Mom did. He greased the fry pan and placed it on the burner. Setting the burner on high, he put two slices of bread into the toaster. He'd watch the toaster closely since it stuck sometimes. Then, he cracked six eggs into the pan. Dad would be hungry after a hard day at work and happy to find supper all ready when he arrived home.

The front doorbell rang. Tony left the kitchen to see who was at the door. A young woman with long, frizzy hair greeted him.

"Hi, is your mom or dad home?" She held a large orange.

"Why?"

"My name is Sandy, and I'm selling fresh fruit from Florida." She pointed to a produce truck parked on the other side of the street. "You can buy boxes of fresh oranges, lemons, or grapefruit for a reasonable price. Do you think your mom or dad might be interested?"

"I don't think so," Tony said. "They don't have a lot of money."

"It's really a bargain, and it's fresh." She flashed him a beautiful smile.

"No. I need to go."

"Maybe if you tasted a sample, you might change your mind."

Tony fidgeted with the doorknob. "No, thanks. I really have to go."

"Please, just try some," Sandy insisted. "It's really sweet and juicy."

"Oh, all right."

Sandy cut a slice of orange for Tony to taste, and it was delicious.

"Isn't it wonderful?" Sandy smiled.

"Yes, but…" Tony sniffed the air. Something inside was burning. "I have to go. My mom and dad aren't home. Goodbye." He slammed the door shut and raced back to the kitchen just in time to hear the smoke alarm go off. Burned toast smoldered, stuck in the toaster, while dark brown eggs smoked in the frying pan.

"Oh, no!" Tony said as he removed the fry pan from the burner and turned off the stove. He pushed the burned toast up and pounded the counter with his fist.

Just then, Dad entered the house from the side door. "What's going on here?" Dad reached up and turned off the smoke detector. "Better turn on the fan, Tony. I'll open the door to help air out the kitchen."

After doing as his dad asked, Tony plunked himself down at the table and stared at his empty plate.

"What happened, Tony? You know better than to leave anything on the stove unattended." Dad's furry eyebrows pushed together.

"I started supper for us. I wanted to surprise you." He sighed. "Then, a girl came to the front door selling fresh fruit. She wouldn't leave, and...then, you came home."

Dad removed his jacket and walked over to Tony.

"I didn't do it on purpose." Tony picked up his fork and poked at the plate. "It was an accident."

"I know." Dad placed his hand on Tony's shoulder. "I understand." He looked Tony in the eye, and his face broke into a wide smile. "Well, you certainly did surprise me."

Tony grinned. "I guess so."

After that ruined meal, Dad did most of the cooking while Mom stayed in New York. Tony helped with other chores, like doing the dishes.

On Saturday, Dad had to work, so Tony thought he'd help by doing the laundry. He had to prove to Dad and himself that he could take care of himself. This time, Dad would be proud of him.

He'd helped Mom before, so Tony thought he knew what to do. After gathering the dirty clothes, he sorted the white clothes into one pile and the colored clothes into another pile. He placed the colored clothes into the washing machine first and poured in the laundry detergent. Wanting the clothes to come out super clean, he added extra detergent.

No mistakes this time, he thought to himself as he answered the phone.

Jed was on the other end of the line. "Hey, Tony. How's it going?"

"Okay, I guess. What's up?"

"Not much."

"I thought you were going to Sheridan today." Tony sat down on a kitchen stool.

"Dad's truck broke down, so we couldn't go."

"My dad had to work today."

"Hope you don't plan on any cooking today. I think the firemen are on vacation." Jed laughed.

"Very funny, Jed." Tony scowled.

"Have you heard from your mom?"

"She called last night. She's flying into Sheridan next Saturday."

"I'll bet it's nice not to have her nagging you all the time."

"Kind of." Tony frowned.

"Kind of? She'd drive me crazy," Jed said.

"At least my mom's coming back," Tony snapped.

"Yeah, right. I gotta go." Jed ended the call.

Why had he snapped at his best friend? He hadn't meant to be so hurtful. Or had he? It was too late now. He'd better check the laundry, but first, he needed to use the bathroom.

After relieving himself, he went to the laundry room. Tony stared at the washer and gasped. Glistening white soap bubbles covered the washer and the dryer, spilling onto the floor. He must be dreaming.

"Tony, what's going on?" Dad stepped up behind him. He placed his hand on his forehead, closed his eyes, and gave a heavy sigh. "As if things weren't going bad enough at work today and now this."

"Dad!" Tony jumped. "What are you doing home?"

"I'm on my lunch break. I wanted to see if you needed anything."

"Well, I thought I'd do some laundry," Tony said. "The phone rang and…"

"Never mind." Dad shook his head. His voice sounded hard and angry. "I can't wait until your mother gets home."

"You won't tell her about this, will you?" Tony pushed his hands deep into his jeans' pockets.

"No. She'd have a fit if she found out." Dad frowned. "I'm beginning to see why she doesn't trust you. You don't think. You're like Joey." Dad was almost yelling now, and Tony felt tears spring to his eyes.

Tony ran to his room and slammed the door. He threw himself onto his bed and buried his face in his pillow. He couldn't do anything right. Dad's words hurt like being punched hard in the gut. Why had Dad compared him to Joey? Joey, the brother nobody talked about. Tony wanted to disappear off the face of the earth.

"Tony," Dad knocked on the bedroom door. "May I come in?"

"No! Go away. Leave me alone."

Dad's voice was soft. "Tony, please. I need to talk to you."

Tony didn't answer.

Dad opened the door and walked in. He sat down on the edge of the bed next to him. "I'm sorry. I didn't really mean what I said. He rubbed his right temple. "It's been a bad morning." His forehead furrowed. "It's just that I'm still upset about Nana's death. And having your mom gone… Try to understand."

"If you really want me to understand, then tell me about Joey."

His dad clasped his hands together and lowered his head. His eyes filled with tears.

"Joey." Dad barely managed to choke out the name. Tony was shocked when Dad kept speaking. "Joey died when he was four. It happened two months before you were born. He was playing in the sandbox in the backyard. Your mom was working in the house. When she called him for lunch, he wasn't there, so she went looking for him." He sighed.

Tony could see how hard this was for his dad. He wanted to tell him that it was all right, he didn't have to tell the story. But his curiosity overpowered him, and he stayed quiet.

"That's when she heard the screech of brakes and a neighbor scream." Dad closed his eyes and breathed deeply. "Joey had wandered away from the yard. He ran into the street…and a man hit him with his truck. And Joey was gone." Dad began to cry. "Your mom blamed herself for not watching him more closely."

Then, with a shudder, Dad broke down and sobbed. Tony sat up and leaned his head on Dad's shoulder. He'd never seen his dad cry. Poor Mom. That explained why she was so protective of him.

Tony sat with Dad for what seemed like a very long time. When Dad wiped away the tears, he looked Tony in the eyes.

"I love you, Tony. Don't ever forget that."

Tony and Dad went back to the laundry room, and together they cleaned up the mess. He'd try to be more careful from now on.

As the rest of the week slowly passed by, Tony thought a lot about what his dad had said. The way Mom treated him made so much more sense to him now. He loved Mom and missed her. But at the same time, he enjoyed having more freedom to do as he pleased. Luckily, Jed seemed to have overlooked what Tony had said on the phone about his mother. Tony guessed Jed understood.

The weather turned ugly the night before Mom's arrival. Like Jed's dad always said, "If you don't like the weather in Wyoming, just wait a few minutes and it will change." As the sky darkened, Tony turned on the radio in the kitchen, hoping to hear that the storm was going to pass quickly and everything would be fine in the morning.

The weatherman forecasted the first blizzard of the season for Montana, Colorado, and Wyoming. High winds gusting up to seventy miles per hour and fourteen inches of snow were predicted. Tony closed his eyes and shuddered. What if…? No, he must not think of the "what ifs."

On Saturday morning, Tony woke to the sound of swirling winds outside his bedroom window. When he opened his eyes, the light seemed brighter than usual. He reached over and pulled the curtain back, but all he could see was the white of a blizzard. The utter whiteness of it was mesmerizing, and Tony found himself staring out the window for several minutes.

Then, he remembered that Mom was flying in today. A sudden sick feeling came over him. What if her flight was canceled? What if she got stranded? Worse yet, what if something happened to her plane? No, he mustn't think like that.

Tony hurriedly dressed and joined Dad a few minutes later in the kitchen.

"Good morning, Tony." Dad stretched and yawned. "I didn't sleep good last night."

"Good morning." Tony fell silent. He hadn't slept good either, but he didn't want to say any of his worries out loud. He didn't want Dad to think he was afraid.

"The weatherman's prediction about a blizzard was right on. Looks nasty outside." Dad ran his large hands through his dark curly hair. "I have a feeling your mom won't be coming home today."

"Don't say that." Tony slammed the bread drawer.

"Take it easy, Tony. I just meant she might have to stay in Denver until the storm lets up, so she won't make the connection to Sheridan." Dad rubbed the back of his neck. "I heard the news this morning, and the storm has shut down a lot of places."

"But what if she gets stuck at the airport?" Tony bit his lower lip.

"Don't worry; your mom can take care of herself. She'll be all right."

Dad was right; there wasn't anything he could do. His mom called later in the day. Snowed in at the Denver airport, she hoped to be home Sunday. Relieved that she at least wouldn't be flying in the blizzard, Tony spent the day watching television, sketching, and reading to pass the time. He tried not to think about Mom or the weather, but the howling wind made it difficult. When the power went out for a couple of hours, he wondered if the storm would ever stop.

On Sunday afternoon, at two degrees below zero, Tony and his dad drove to the Sheridan airport. Interstate 90 had been cleared, but slick spots remained. A sheer blue sky draped itself behind the snowy peaks. Tony stared at the whiteness that seemed to go on forever.

"Do you remember the time your mom sat on the cake?" Dad adjusted the heater.

Tony laughed as the memory flashed in his mind. "How could I forget? She was as mad as a hornet." He tugged on his seatbelt.

"I tried to warn her, but she was in a tizzy about something."

"Remember the time Mom found a beetle in her soup?" Tony grinned. "I thought she was going to go crazy."

Dad stretched his shoulders. "So did everyone in the restaurant. I wanted to laugh, but I didn't dare."

"Me, too." Tony chuckled. "I miss Mom. I'm glad she's coming home."

"So do I." Dad glanced over at Tony and smiled. "Your mom's a character. I guess that's why I love her so much."

The traffic in front of them slowed down. Tony saw the flashing red and blue lights from two police cars and an ambulance. A semitrailer had jackknifed and blocked the right lane of the interstate. Two other cars were wedged into a snow bank on the side of the road next to the truck.

"Wow!" Tony said. "What a mess! Can we get by?" He fidgeted in his seat. "We can't be late to pick up Mom."

"I'm not sure. The traffic seems to be funneling through the left lane." Dad tapped his fingers on the steering wheel. He peered to the left, trying to see past the rows of cars, focused on the road ahead. "It's moving slowly, but it's moving."

Tony stared at the wreck as they passed by. "Do you suppose anybody got killed?"

"I don't know. I hope not." Dad sighed. "Icy roads are so dangerous."

Tony felt better knowing the weather had cleared in Denver. His mom had sounded excited on the phone when she talked to him that morning to let them know she would be heading home on the next flight.

The Sheridan airport was small. Tony and Dad waited outside in the frosty air by the chain link fence for the plane to arrive. Inside the terminal, a man at the counter had told him the plane should be landing at any moment. Tony searched the sky until he spotted a glint of silver moving toward the airport.

"I see it!" Tony said with breath of frosty air.

"Me, too."

The glint of silver turned into a small plane as it approached the runway. Tony didn't have to worry anymore. In a few minutes, Mom would be safe on the ground.

The plane lifted back up into the air.

"Dad!" Tony grabbed the chain link fence and squeezed it hard.

"Something's wrong." Dad clenched his gloved hands.

The plane began circling the airport.

"Dad, what's wrong?"

Dad's face turned an ashen gray. He took a deep breath but didn't say anything.

For some reason, the plane couldn't land. Maybe it was the landing gear. If it didn't work, the plane would surely crash, and Mom might be killed. Tony grabbed Dad's arm at the blare of the fire truck sirens and the flashing lights of an ambulance. He watched them hurry out to the runway.

"Everything's going to be all right, Tony." Dad hugged him. "It's going to be all right."

Tony and Dad watched the plane circle repeatedly. People scurried about the airport as police cars pulled up in front. Some reporters arrived with their cameras ready.

"What's happening?" Dad asked one of the policemen.

"The report said the landing gear is jammed. It won't open all the way."

Tony's stomach churned with fear. Why this plane? Everything seemed to be happening so fast, but the plane seemed to circle forever. Mom must be terrified. So many terrible thoughts crossed his mind. Would he end up without a mom, like Jed?

The plane began to descend again. Tony held his breath as the shiny metal bird lowered itself from the sky.

He strained to see the landing gear. *Please let it be down*, he thought to himself. Suddenly, he felt like he was going to throw up, but then he saw the wheels lower from the belly of the plane. The landing gear worked, and the plane glided toward the runway. The wheels touched the ground.

"Whoo!" Tony sighed in relief. He watched the plane speed down the runway. Then, without warning, one of the wheels collapsed and sent the plane into a spin. He gasped as the plane spun around and skidded for what seemed like forever. It jerked to a halt with its nose and left wing down at the end of the runway.

"She's going to be all right. Isn't she, Dad?" Tony shouted.

All Dad could do was hold Tony tight.

With sirens blaring, the fire trucks and ambulances raced out to the plane. Firemen scurried onto the scene in a bustle of activity as passengers were removed from the wrecked plane. Tony searched for any sign of his mother.

An announcement called all people awaiting passengers from flight 274 to come to the terminal. Tony and his dad hurried in with the other people waiting for loved ones. Soon, passengers were brought into the airport terminal.

Men hugged wives, parents hugged children, and friends greeted friends. Reporters took pictures.

There had been no serious injuries. When Mom saw Tony and Dad, she ran to them and nearly knocked them over. She hugged and kissed Dad and turned to Tony.

"Tony, Tony," she said. "I'll never leave you again."

Deadly Wings

Tony was a prisoner. Mom had meant it when she said she'd never leave him again. All winter, ever since that day at the airport, his mom refused to let him go anywhere or do anything. She seemed to panic if he went down a different aisle in the grocery store.

Despite not being able to go anywhere, Tony and Jed became best friends. They spent a lot of time on the playground together at recess, and sometimes Jed spent the weekend with him, but Tony couldn't do anything away from home unless Mom came with him.

School would be out in a couple of weeks. Tony dreaded the thought of not seeing Jed every day, but he wouldn't miss Regina. After the window-painting incident, Regina had picked on him even more. She'd cut in front of him in the lunch line, knock his books off the desk, or make faces at him when Mr. Brunswick wasn't looking.

On Friday, Ms. Shadbolt substituted for Mr. Brunswick, and all the kids disliked her. Ms. Shadbolt had a tiny head with beady eyes and always puckered her lips. She had a habit of clearing her throat with a pig-like grunt.

"Who can find the country of France on the world map?" Ms. Shadbolt stood with her pointer stick by the world map in front of the room.

Tony raised his hand.

"You, the boy with the mop of brown hair." Ms. Shadbolt pointed to Tony. "Come up."

Tony walked up to the map and placed his finger on France.

"That's correct. Now who can find England?"

Tony walked back to his desk and sat down. Regina grinned at him. His bottom felt wet. He looked down. A blob of white glue oozed beneath him.

Yuck! What now? If the teacher called on him again, what would he do? What if he stuck to the chair? Tony tried to wipe it off with a tissue he found from inside his desk. He glared at Regina who sat with a smirk on her face. Tony wished he could just fly out the window into the morning blue sky. He wanted to join the birds and buzzing bees. If only the recess bell would ring …

"You." Ms. Shadbolt pointed to Tony. "Come here. I need you to take this note to the office."

"Me?" Tony swallowed hard.

"Yes. You."

Tony stood. Maybe if he kept his backside away from Ms. Shadbolt, she wouldn't notice. The class snickered as he shuffled toward the teacher's desk. Ms. Shadbolt studied him.

"What's going on here?" She asked with her hands on her hips. "What are you hiding behind your back?"

"Nothing, Ms. Shadbolt." Tony fidgeted. He held out his hands for her to see.

"Look at his bottom." Regina laughed.

"Turn around. Let me see," Ms. Shadbolt ordered. "Oh my!" Then, she stood and turned on Regina. "You're responsible for this, aren't you? I knew you were up to something." She marched over to Regina.

Regina squirmed in her desk. "Me? I didn't..."

"Don't lie to me, young lady. I'm no fool," she grunted. "You will stay inside during recess, and you will clean off this young man's chair."

By the time Tony wiped off his jeans and returned to the classroom, everyone had gone to recess. Ms. Shadbolt tromped past him, headed for the restrooms. He noticed Regina sitting statue-like at her desk. She stared at him with melon-sized eyes.

Tony walked toward her desk by the window. Powder-white fear masked her face.

"Regina, what's wrong?" Tony bit his lower lip. Why didn't she move?

Regina didn't answer. She lowered her eyes toward her arm where wasp wings shimmered as the insect crawled up her forearm. Tony winced.

"Don't move, and it won't sting you," Tony edged closer.

Ever since he'd been stung on the neck by a bee at a picnic, he hated bees or wasps—anything that stung.

Tony waited. He could hear the loud, steady click of the classroom clock on the wall behind him. The smell of fumes from a passing truck wafted through the window into the room. If he waited, the wasp would fly away. He watched Regina. Beads of sweat began to glisten on her thick eyebrows. The wasp continued to ramble over the fine blond hair on her arm.

"Why don't you brush it off?" Tony frowned.

"I'm allergic." Regina seemed to force the words from deep inside. "I could die. Please, get it off me."

The look on Regina's face and the sound of her voice frightened him. This wasn't the Regina he knew. He had to act quickly, so he grabbed a notebook from a desk. What if he missed and the wasp stung her?

"Get it off. Get it off."

He had to admit it felt good to be in control of Regina, but he didn't really want her to die. Tony raised the notebook and with one swat knocked the wasp off her arm. Regina popped out of her seat. The wasp flew into the air above Tony and buzzed around his head. He swatted at it again. The angry wasp zoomed toward his face.

"Get it!" Regina shouted as she ducked low.

Tony tried again, and this time he knocked it to the floor. He rushed up to the buzzing menace and squashed it beneath his shoe.

Regina shuddered.

Tony took a deep breath and stared at Regina.

"You won't tell anyone?" Regina shook. "You know, about me being scared." She gazed at the floor. "My dad would be angry. He doesn't want me to be afraid of anything."

Tony rubbed the sticky remains of the wasp off his shoe onto the floor.

"No, I won't tell." Tony stared at Regina. She didn't look so big anymore.

Regina clasped her hands together. "Tony," she said in a soft voice.

"What?"

"Sorry about the glue."

Tony shrugged his shoulders and left the room. For the first time, he thought Regina meant it.

After school, Tony hurried home. Somehow, he knew Regina wouldn't bother him anymore. The thought made him smile. The smile faded as he saw Mom waiting for him on the doorstep, ready to greet him with a hug.

"How's my little Tony?"

"Mom, I'm not your little Tony. How many times do I have to tell you?"

Mom ignored the question. "I made your favorite oatmeal cookies today." She walked into the kitchen.

Tony followed her, placed his books on the counter, and sat down at the table. Mom placed a platter of cookies before him and poured him a cold glass of milk. Tony took a big gulp.

"Thanks. It's sure hot today."

"Sticky. Reminds me of living in New York." Mom wiped her forehead with a tissue. "I don't feel very good today."

Tony noticed the sunlight fade as he bit into a cookie.

"Is it supposed to rain today?" Tony licked a crumb from the corner of his mouth. "It's getting cloudy."

"Chance of thunderstorms. We could use a good rain to green up the front lawn."

"Mom, Jed asked me if I could go fishing with him this weekend."

"I don't know, Tony. Where?" Mom picked at something dried on the counter with her thumbnail.

"Sherd Lake. It's not far." Tony brushed some cookie crumbs off the table.

"But, Tony, you promised to help me in the garden." Mom's forehead wrinkled.

"I'll help you next weekend. I promise." Tony crossed his heart. "Besides, Jed and I haven't done anything together in a long time."

"I don't know. The weather could change, and you could get caught in one of those nasty mountain storms." Mom clasped her hands nervously.

"Mom, I could get caught in a storm walking home from school."

"True, but…"

"But, what?"

Mom pushed back a wisp of hair from her face and looked out the window. She stared out the window for a moment and then turned to Tony.

"No." She wiped her forehead again. "I need your help in the garden *this* weekend. It's almost the end of May, and I need to get the vegetables planted."

"But, Mom …"

"No, and I don't want to hear another word about it." Her face tightened.

Tony glared at her. Would she ever learn to trust him?

"You never let me do anything," he grumbled. He grabbed his books and stormed off to his bedroom. How was he ever going to grow up?

Wedge of Fear

Hot heavy air weighed on Tony and made sweat trickle down his face. He opened his bedroom window wider, not even a hint of a breeze. An early darkness settled in the sky, and Tony flicked on the light switch. He sat down at his desk, took out a sheet of notebook paper, and opened his math book.

"Tony, come here. Hurry! Listen to this," Mom called from the kitchen.

Tony raced to the kitchen.

"We have a weather bulletin," the radio announcer said. "A tornado watch has been issued for Johnson, Big Horn, and Sheridan counties until eight o'clock tonight. Please stay tuned for further updates."

Great. Just what Mom needed—something else to worry about. He couldn't remember ever having a tornado watch in New York. Tony wiped his sweaty brow with the back of his hand. If he remembered correctly from his science class, a tornado watch meant the possibility of a tornado, and a warning meant an actual sighting of one.

Thunder rumbled close by. Again, he walked over to the window and peered out. Dark billowy clouds threatened. Tony bit his lower lip. Did he need to worry?

By the time Tony finished his math assignment, thunder boomed louder. A cool breeze pushed the curtains, and rain spattered his window. He shut his math book, closed the window, and then hurried into the living room. Mom lay on the faded sofa in the darkened room in her favorite quilt, an open magazine by her side. Even in the dim light, Tony noticed her pale face.

"Tony, would you please turn on the light? It's getting so dark," she said in a worried voice. "And close my bedroom window. It's starting to rain."

He turned a lamp on, closed the bedroom windows, and then walked back into the living room. Tony tapped his fingers on the wall.

"Would you mind having leftovers tonight?" Mom winced. "I'm not feeling good."

"No, that's okay." Tony wiped his sweaty palms on his jeans. "Is there any mac and cheese?"

"I think so." Mom rubbed her left shoulder.

BAROOM BOOM BOOM! Tony jumped and knocked into the lampshade. The storm had decided to release its angry surge of energy. Lightning flashed repeatedly, and rain pounded the roof like heavy footsteps. The trees swayed and groaned.

"I wish your dad hadn't driven over the mountain to Worland today. I'm not sure when he'll be back." Mom breathed heavily and rubbed her shoulder even harder.

"What's wrong, Mom?" Tony perched on top of the coffee table in front of the sofa.

"I don't know. I have a pain in my shoulder." She flinched.

"Mom, the weatherman said we have a tornado watch until eight o'clock tonight," Tony blurted. He shouldn't have reminded her.

His mom furrowed her brow. "I know." Mom continued to rub her left shoulder. She grimaced. "What should we do? Quick, turn up the kitchen radio!"

"Mom, it's just a watch," Tony said, but deep inside he knew there was reason to worry.

"Tony, we don't even have a basement for protection." Mom leaned forward and groaned.

"Mom, what is it?"

Another jolt of piercing white illuminated the room, followed by an instant crashing boom.

"I'm all right," she mumbled. "Go turn up the radio!"

Tony turned up the radio. The familiar sound of a song by one of his mom's favorite music groups, the Beatles, poured into the room. Suddenly, he heard the clattering sound of hail pelting the house. It grew louder and then almost deafening. Another bolt of lightning flashed, followed by an instant explosion of thunder.

A BEEP BEEP BEEP interrupted the music. "WARNING! A tornado has been sighted on the ground just south of Buffalo. All residents are advised to take immediate cover. I repeat, immediate—"

A tremendous boom interrupted the broadcast.

"Tony! Tony! The pain in my arm is worse. Help me."

Tony rushed into the living room and knelt next to his mom. He looked at her pale, sweaty face. Tears filled her eyes, and her fists were clenched.

"Mom, we need to get next door to the neighbor's basement." He stood. "Now!"

"I can't." Mom's face contorted in pain as she gasped for air. "I think I'm having a heart attack."

A heart attack? Of course. Why hadn't he recognized the signs? He should have known this from his first aid class.

The lights went out. Tony looked out the window just as a tree carved a neighbor's garage in half.

Tony's mind began to spin. Nana had died from a heart attack. He bit his lower lip hard. What should he do? A heart attack! A tornado! He'd call 911.

He raced to the kitchen telephone and picked it up. The phone was dead! The telephone lines must be down. Why didn't his parents have cell phones like everyone else? He reached into his pocket. Where was his iPhone? No time to look for it.

"Tony!" Mom screamed, as a huge cottonwood limb burst through the living room window scattering shards of glass everywhere. The wind howled through the house, tearing everything off the walls and upsetting lamps and small pieces of furniture. Tony heard the sound of splintering wood and shingles being ripped from the roof.

Tony ran to his mom's side. A cold gust of rain and wind slapped him in the face. The leaves and small branches of the broken tree limb clawed at his mom, who cowered on the corner of the sofa. They scratched and scraped on the walls and furniture.

"Mom!"

Splinters of shattered glass covered her. Blood trickled down her wide-eyed face. The angry wind shouted at him.

Suddenly, a wedge of fear cut between him and Mom. The fear of death, his and Mom's, stared him in the face. A wedge of fear that tore him apart, leaving him frozen in two. He wanted to run for shelter, save himself, but he couldn't move. He wanted to save his mom, take care of her, but he couldn't.

"Tony, help me," Mom's voice pleaded as she held her hand out to him.

If he could only take that first step—but his feet were rooted in the carpet. Like in a nightmare, he couldn't breathe or move. He was suspended in a time zone of terror; seeing, hearing, and feeling. Stuck. Caught. Wrapped in an invisible web of horror.

Another bolt of lightning and a surge of power unknown to him took hold of his mind and body. "Move!" a voice screamed from deep within. The fear shattered and jolted him into action.

"Mom! We've got to get next door!" He reached out and pulled Mom to her feet, wrapping the quilt around her shoulders. "Put your arm around my neck and lean on me."

Tony and Mom staggered toward the front door. Hail pelted them. He had to get Mom to a basement, but it was too late. Tony heard what sounded like the roar of a freight train. The tornado was almost upon them. Mom screamed and bent over. Tony saw the black spiraling monster coming toward the house. It swayed like the tail of an angry dragon, an evil sky serpent sucking up life, wiping away everything in its path.

What now? The bathroom would be the next safest place to go. A blast of cold air and breaking sounds followed him down the hall. With just seconds to spare, Tony slammed the door with all his might behind him and helped his mom get into the bathtub. He covered Mom and himself with the quilt and prayed.

"Tony, I'm so scared." Mom shivered in the cold.

"Hang on, Mom."

What if Mom died? What if he died? Why was this happening?

A deafening roar engulfed him and drowned out Mom's screams. The world around him exploded. The storm bulldozed the roof away, and the bathroom walls shuddered and splintered apart. The medicine cabinet ripped off the wall, shattering the mirror and scattering glass everywhere. Parts of the ceiling began to collapse, showering him with boards and insulation. The tub shook violently as the force of the wind wrenched everything around him.

Household objects hurtled through the air, and golf ball-sized hail pounded his back. Grinding, banging, crashing sounds whirled about him. The tornado sucked up the contents of the house and then spilled its guts everywhere. Death called to him.

In an instant, it was over. Tony lifted his head. No roof. No walls. Only a light drizzle.

"I can't move...the pain..." Mom gasped.

"I'm going to get help."

Tony stumbled his way through the wreckage of what had once been his house. The refrigerator lay on its side. The sofa had been replaced by a doghouse. He rushed into the street and tripped on the scattered bricks of a chimney. Overturned cars, tattered clothing, and broken furniture littered the street. Downed electrical wires crackled by pretzel-twisted tree trunks. Bloodied people began to rise up out of the debris. A soaked, long-haired cat meowed loudly.

Stunned, Tony saw only skeletons of the houses that had once lined his side of the street. He started toward his neighbor's house across the street. Mr. Taylor ran up to Tony.

"Are you all right?" Mr. Taylor asked. "Can I help?"

"Mom," Tony said. "It's my mom. She's having a heart attack."

"I'll call for help." Mr. Taylor wiped blood from a cut above his eye. "You stay with your mom. I'll be right back."

Tony found Mom moaning in pain. She needed to be kept warm, but everything around him was soaked.

"Mom, you're going to be okay. Mr. Taylor's calling for help."

Tony closed his eyes for a moment, trying to make the nightmare go away, but it didn't. Where was the ambulance? Maybe it couldn't get through because of the debris. Every minute seemed like an hour. He noticed his arm was bleeding, and a gash above his elbow began to sting.

With the blare of a siren, help arrived. The ambulance attendants placed his mom on a stretcher. Tony jumped when one of the EMTs slipped, jarring Mom into a loud groan. Mr. Taylor stood by with his hand on Tony's shoulder. Just as the ambulance sped off, Tony heard his name.

"Tony! Tony!" He turned to see Dad racing up to him with wide eyes. "Are you hurt?"

"Dad!" Tony hugged Dad and broke into tears. "Mom had a heart attack."

"Is she all right?" Dad stood back and searched Tony's eyes. Stress lines fractured his face.

"The ambulance just took her to the hospital," Mr. Taylor said.

"Tony, follow me back to the car. I know it's dangerous, but we need to get over to the hospital." Dad brushed off the drizzle that was covering his forehead. Tony hurriedly followed but was careful to avoid getting injured by the debris scattered everywhere.

At the hospital, the emergency room bustled with a flurry of doctors and nurses helping storm victims. Tony's mom had been placed in the intensive care unit. The doctor reported that she had had a heart attack but was now resting comfortably. Tony's shoulders dropped with a sigh of relief. Mom was going to make it.

Tony sat next to his Dad in the waiting room after a nurse had cleaned and bandaged his arm. He told Dad everything that had happened.

"Anthony Eugene Greco, you're a hero. You saved your mom's life." Dad leaned back in the chair. "You did a lot of growing up today."

"Excuse me, Mr. Greco," a nurse said. "You and your son may visit your wife now. She's in the second room of the ICU, straight down the end of this hallway." She smiled and hurried off.

Tony and Dad walked down the crowded hall to the intensive care unit. It smelled of disinfectant. Tony cringed at the sight of all the tubes and wires attached to Mom. The monitors made strange beeping sounds. Mom extended her hand as Tony approached the side of her bed.

"Hi, Mom." Tony grasped her cold hand.

"How are you doing, sweetheart?" Dad brushed a wisp of hair away from Mom's face and kissed her forehead.

"I'm alive—thanks to Tony." Tears welled up in her eyes.

"Don't cry, Mom." He rubbed his hands on his jeans. If she cried, he would, too.

"Tony, I'm so proud of you." Mom sniffled. "You're not a little boy anymore."

A nurse poked her head in the door and suggested they keep the visit short.

"Well, we'd better go. Tony and I have a lot to do. You left the house in sort of a mess." Dad gave a small smile, the first one Tony had seen on his face since the tornado had hit.

"How can you joke about the house?" A single tear leaked out of the corner of her eye.

"Well, you can replace a house, but not the people you love. Don't worry. Things will work out," Dad said. He placed his arm around Tony's shoulder.

Mom squeezed Tony's hand. "You're right."

"Mom?"

"Yes, Tony."

"Do you think I can go fishing sometime soon with Jed?

Mom gave a small, watery smile and then winked. "That will depend on the weather."

Discussion Questions for *Wedge of Fear*

1. How do you think Tony feels about his move to Wyoming at the beginning of the story?
2. What do you think Tony misses the most about leaving New York?
3. What kind of a teacher is Mr. Brunswick?
4. How are Tony and Jed different?
5. Why do you think Jed and Tony become friends?
6. Why do you think Regina bullies Tony?
7. How would you describe Jed's Aunt Billie?
8. What are the things Tony fears?
9. How does Tony feel about his mother?
10. How do you think Tony feels at the end of the story?

Acknowledgments

I want to thank Patricia Landy for believing in my writing ability and for being so encouraging. Special thanks to my wife Carol, my children, and many friends for their love and support since the very beginning.

About the Author

Born and raised in Niagara Falls, New York, Gene—like his main character Tony—understands the culture shock of moving from the East to Wyoming. Gene knew he had to live out West after traveling there with a summer camp upon college graduation. He and his wife Carol have four children, six grandchildren, two cats, Sitsi and Buster, and a dog named Annie, a golden retriever/chow mix. Gene enjoys reading and writing, hiking in the Big Horn Mountains, singing tenor in the community choir, painting acrylic landscapes, and spending hours in both his flower and vegetable gardens. Known by many as *the teacher who dances on his desk*, Gene has a great sense of humor and a sweet tooth. To learn more about the author go to www.gargene.com.